The Lobster Rode in on a Bicycle:

My Jamaica Hideaway

Alice Rainich Nichols

The Lobster Rode in on a Bicycle: My Jamaica Hideaway

Artwork, cover design,
and preparation for publication by
Susan Vaughn Turner

Nonfiction / Family / Memoir / Jamaica / Caribbean / Travel

ISBN: 1483981495
ISBN-13: 978-1483981499

For Vera,
wherever she might be ...

With thanks to the Jamaican People;
my daughter Kathy for her
support, input, and encouragement;
and to Susan Turner,
without whom this book would not exist.

CONTENTS

I. Jamaica

   1. The Lobster Rode in on a Bicycle — 1

   2. Jericho — 10

   3. Herman — 16

   4. Vera — 19

   5. Fox and Willow — 25

   6. The Crusty Curmudgeon — 31

   7. Peacocks — 40

   8. Mr. Sevens — 50

   9. Exchange — 56

  10. Hector Duncan — 60

II. Out of Many, One People

  11. Out of Many, One People — 67

  12. Patois — 71

  13. Cricket, Lovely Cricket — 78

  14. Braid Yer Hair, Lady? — 84

  15. The Gleaner — 88

III. Living in the Upton Manner

  16. Living in the Upton Manner — 95

  17. The Sound and the Fury — 102

  18. John Collier: The Czar of Upton — 110

  19. Water, Water, Everywhere — 116

  20. The Campbells Are Coming, Hooray, Hooray — 121

  21. Jamaica Farewell I: Early Mornin' Tea — 128

  22. Jamaica Farewell II: Won't Be Back for Many a Day — 139

I. Jamaica

1 THE LOBSTER
RODE in on a BICYCLE

Unlike that lonely yellow bird, there were six of us lounging about on the veranda and by the pool at 'Villa Sundowner.'   The sun was down and the 'Runaway Rhythm Boys' were playing the wonderful old Calypsos for us. Janney had finally gotten it across to Bingo, the leader of the small combo, that what we REALLY wanted to hear were the traditional, familiar Calypsos such as *Linstead Market*, *Brownskin Gal* and Janney's particular favorite, *Cricket, Lovely Cricket*, that were known throughout the Caribbean; not this band's version of faded American songs from the 30's--*Red Sails in the Sunset* or *Slow Boat to China*, which they'd played on the evening of our arrival.

* * * * * * *

1

Janney and I, along with our teenaged twins Kathy and Mike, each with a friend they'd invited, had piled into an ancient taxi at the airport in Montego Bay, and since our luggage had failed to arrive, all six of us were able to squeeze in, but just barely. "Soon come!" said Cascade, the driver, when we told him about the bags, and sure enough, we were awakened the very next morning by a truck that came roaring into the driveway of the vacation villa we'd rented. Our six suitcases were dropped off and the truck roared away again. We would stay for eight more glorious days before the kids had to be back in college. Janney and I would leave for our respective jobs two days later.

Quickly pulling on our swimsuits that first morning in Jamaica, we were off to the beach in the rental car we'd found parked in the driveway--part of the villa deal. Happily, it was a much newer model than Cascade's decades old rust-bucket. The beach, just five minutes away, was practically deserted; turquoise waves lapped up onto pristine, sugar white sand while palm trees swayed gently in the breeze along the shores of the cove. It looked exactly like a brochure at a travel agency. The kids ran and dove into the water while Janney and I lathered up with sunblock, wanting to soak up as much sun as we dared on this first day. This setting was quite different from the wintry scene we'd left in Ann Arbor the day before.

* * * * * * *

Happy as we had been to be back in the States after eighteen years of living as expats in the tropics, we had more than a few misgivings. It was cold in Michigan! There was a lot of snow! The children had never seen snow before but the novelty soon wore off when they had flu during the whole Christmas vacation. Janney complained about having to shovel the driveway; while I, who had been so looking forward to ice skating (I'd practically lived on ice skates as a kid), couldn't even make it onto the ice, so wobbly were my ankles.

After one season of braving it we decided that the following year we'd take our annual vacation in the winter and go to Barbados where we'd sometimes spent our 'short leaves' while still living in Venezuela.

Unfortunately we waited too long before doing anything about it and our favorite Barbados hotel, The Paradise Beach Club, was booked solid for that entire winter. But then our brother-in-law Jim, whose work took him all over the Caribbean, came up with a place he knew in Jamaica. We could have it for the ten days after Christmas, which was perfect, falling between semesters for the kids who were now freshmen in college.

* * * * * * *

Late on the afternoon of December 26th, Cascade pulled his creaking taxicab into the driveway of the four bedroom, three bath Vacation Villa. A staff of three came out to greet us: Linda, who introduced herself as cook/ housekeeper, while Lenore the housemaid and Dazzel--the gardener/pool boy followed suit. There were cold drinks, Linda told us, and dinner would be ready at seven. This sounded wonderful! Already beginning to relax, I could smell chicken roasting in the kitchen.

Janney and I agreed that we didn't understand the 'Villa' concept at all. Was Sundowner the home of Jim's friends who would just be away for the holidays? We'd assumed we would be going to a restaurant for dinner that evening and hadn't even thought about further meal arrangements. But Linda explained that groceries were on hand for tonight's meal as well as for breakfast, and that we could shop at Miss Taylor's, a small grocery store nearby, to buy food for subsequent meals, which she, Linda, would be preparing for us.

Meanwhile Janney and the boys had found the small supply of cold beer and were digging in; they were ALMOST eighteen, after all! The girls and I, in the absence of swimsuits, had draped ourselves sarong style in bath towels over our undies, unwilling to miss even one golden ray before the sun set, while Janney and the boys set off in search of more beer. Clearly the six bottles they'd found would not last out the night. The girls and I finally gave up on the sun and changed into shorts while the boys brought in the case of beer they'd bought at Miss Taylors'. Just then

BINGO AND THE
RUNAWAY RHYTHM BOYS

Bingo and his group arrived. Janney offered the band members each a beer. They gladly accepted and asked for another.

Besides Bingo, who sang and shook maracas, the band included Dazzel's father, who played the banjo; Opie, a school boy on the guitar; and Luther, who was now making overtures to Lenore, played the rhumba box. (A rhumba box is actually an ordinary crate with a 6 or 8" round hole cut out of one side. The player sits on the crate and twangs the metal strips that are attached to extend part way over the opening; or else he simply pounds on the box with his hands.) Luther earned his living as a fisherman. Bingo's day job was caddying at the Runaway Bay Golf Course.

Noticing that empties from Jamaica's excellent Red Stripe beer were accumulating at an alarming rate, I asked Lenore if there was a deposit on the bottles. "Oh no, Mizz Nik," she said, her dark face clouding. "I'm sure dey sterilizes dem at de fac'try!"

*　*　*　*　*　*　*

One afternoon, feeling I had already had as much sun as I needed that day, I dropped off Janney and the kids at the beach and headed over to the Runaway Bay Beach Hotel. I'd heard that they had good deals on cashmere sweaters and I had my heart set on a sea foam green cardigan. Entering the Free Port Gift Shop just off the lobby, I asked the man behind the counter what colors and sizes were available. "Just tell me what you want," he replied. "A sea foam green cardigan in a medium size." "Afraid I don't have that" he countered, "what would be your next choice?" "Well, what sizes do you have, or maybe there'd be a pullover?" "Just tell me what you want," he maintained. I ran through my entire hierarchy, always with the same result. It turned out he had exactly one sweater, in black, in a small size.

Just then I noticed that attached to the far end of the lobby was a room, roofed, but otherwise entirely glassed in on three sides. It extended out onto the beach and inside it sat four middle-aged ladies, each draped in a mink stole or fur scarf. They were playing cards in air-conditioned splendor. 'What was the point?' I wondered. They could just as well be in Iowa or Connecticut. Probably their husbands were out, sweating, on the golf course.

As I turned to leave I saw a couple we'd met while going through customs on arrival. They had told us they were hoping to go horseback riding, but now the young man in a booth marked 'RIDING,' was telling them this would not be possible today. "Why not?" asked the visitors. "The horses are sick," he responded. "All of them? How many are there?" they asked. "Forty-seven," came the reply. "And they are ALL sick?" asked the couple, incredulous. "Yes, but they will be alright tomorrow."

I was beginning to learn something of the vagaries of life in Jamaica.

* * * * * * *

And so the days sped by; the kids would be leaving in the morning. I wanted to have a seafood dinner for their last night there, so I asked Linda where we could buy lobsters. "Dere's a beach down by 'Rye'n'vo' a few miles down the road where de boats comes in in the mornin'. You could try dere." Janney and I drove over to what turned out to be Rio Nuevo, where we saw an old fisherman spreading his nets to dry. He pointed to some little specks on the horizon, saying, "Dem be de fishin' boats. When dem comes in you wi' have you lobstah." But when we returned later that morning those specks were still just specks on the horizon. Disappointed, we turned to leave. We had nearly reached the car when the old man caught up with us and tapped Janney on the shoulder. "You lobstah, Sa-ar," he announced proudly. "But how did they get here? The boats are still far away." The old fisherman pointed to a small boy, riding away down the road on a bicycle. We enjoyed a wonderful sea-food dinner and the four kids flew home the next morning.

*   *   *   *   *

That same day we received a phone call from Janney's mother, Kathryn,

WHEN THE *LOBSTAH* BOATS COME IN.

reminding us that their old family friends, George and Betty Eustace, lived just a few miles away in Ocho Rios. Janney phoned the Eustaces and they invited us to lunch the next day, suggesting that we bring bathing suits and meet them by the Esso station on the edge of town and follow them to their home. It's a good thing. We never would have found them otherwise on the narrow, winding road to their home in Upton.

Runaway Bay, named for the place where escaped or freed slaves would depart, is rather flat and sandy and there isn't much there. Just a handful of vacation villas, a hotel and a golf course. Ocho Rios, on the other hand, is actually a town, with shops and banks and many leafy trees besides the coconut palms that grow everywhere on the island.

The Eustaces had a lovely home with a pool and a

large, shaded veranda overlooking the Upton Golf Course and the blue Caribbean beyond. We had a swim and were enjoying a drink before lunch when Janney mentioned that we were interested in the Villa concept, but didn't understand it. George, an engineer, explained it in great detail. One could purchase and own a fully furnished, staffed 'Vacation Villa,' and rent it to vacationers such as ourselves, taking it over for one's own holidays as one chose, sort of like a Caribbean version of a time-share. George then mentioned, casually, that as a matter of fact, there was just such a villa for sale up the road. Guests (renters) were staying there, but they were leaving the next day. We were leaving the day after that. Janney said that we were interested, asking George where we could find the owner. "You're looking at him," said George, grinning.

We had saved up some money during our eighteen years in Venezuela, and obviously it was burning a hole in Janney's pocket. To make a long story a little bit shorter: we bought the place the next day. Bingo and his band showed up at Sundowner that evening and once more played 'Yellow Bird', this time over the telephone to our kids in Ann Arbor, who then heard we were the proud owners of villa we had scarcely seen.

"Yellow Bird, up high in ba-naa-na tree, Yellow Bird, sits all alone like me . . . " And we flew home the next day.

2 JERICHO

We officially took possession of our villa on April 1, 1970, but for a variety of reasons were unable to return to Jamaica until January of the following year. The villa, though actually a duplex, could also be used as one large house with four bedrooms and four baths. It came complete, not only with its pool and furniture, but with linens, dishes, flatware and glasses, which I would gradually replace. There was a staff: a cook/housekeeper, Vera; and a one-eyed knave, the gardener/pool man who was named Herman; both of whom we as owners were free to hire or fire as we chose. We also had the option to retain the services of Mrs. Kirstie Beaton, an elderly Scottish woman who would oversee the property; paying the staff, taking care of bills and the like. We were delighted to leave these matters in her capable hands and opened a joint checking account with her that very same day.

The villa also came complete with a name, *Jericho*. A house name is very important in an area where there are no street numbers and, in many cases, no street names. There was a reason our house was named Jericho and this is how it came about ... The Eustaces and another couple had conceived the idea of a weekend getaway home in Upton while on a visit with friends on Jamaica's north coast. Both couples were expats living in Kingston and had so enjoyed leaving behind the hot and dusty capital that they decided to build a place for themselves near the golf course. They planned the duplex together, the families calling their respective components 'Hook' and 'Slice.'

Inevitably there was a disagreement, followed by a falling out, and it ended with the Eustaces buying out the other couple. They cut a doorway between the two adjoining kitchens thus making the place available as either one large house or two separate apartments. The place was renamed 'Jericho' when that portion of the doorway wall came 'tumblin' down.' When George retired they put Jericho up for sale and built a new, one family home, 'Belle Aire,' a bit closer to the golf course.

* * * * * * *

On arriving at Jericho that January, we attempted in the space of three weeks to freshen up its appearance with new curtains and bedspreads. The house was attractively furnished with white wrought–iron, glass topped tables, round sisal rugs and sofas and chairs with cushions covered in lime green or aqua. I had brought with us bedspreads, a different color for each bedroom, and would now select matching fabrics from the beautiful prints available in shops in Ocho Rios.

Jericho's two verandas were a different matter entirely. Here too were chairs and sofas as well as glass topped tables, but the wrought-iron was a faded salmon color, not the black or white I consider suitable for a tropical décor (verdigris might have been nice for the Mediterranean, but not the Caribbean, in my humble opinion). The chairs and sofas on the verandas had been upholstered in dark green Naugahyde or leatherette, which had seen better days. The seats were discolored by chlorine from numerous wet bathing suits; some of the seams had burst open revealing yellowed cotton batting or thick, crumbling foam rubber.

This situation called for immediate action in the form of a trip to Seow & Sons in Ocho Rios, or 'Hochi,' as it was referred to by the local populace.

"You goin' to Hochi, Mizz Nick? Please, I'm beggin' you, bring me back one ice pick," asked Vera as I left.

Seow & Sons was a wonderful emporium, owned and operated by a Chinese family. At that time in the early

1970s, going into Seow's was like entering a cave. The store has long since been converted into a more or less modern shop, but in both its incarnations it has carried a mixed line of groceries, hardware, dry goods, clothing, china, glassware, liquor, patent medicines and some appliances. In the old days, entering the shop from the street, you stepped up onto a concrete slab that teetered slightly before you descended into the dim interior, carefully ducking beneath a row of pink plastic chamber-pots of various sizes which hung from a wire over the doorway. As your eyes adjusted from the brilliant sunlight outdoors to semidarkness, you could make out counters piled high with various commodities; more boxes littered the aisles. A gleaming, though somewhat dusty white commode partially blocked entrance to the hardware section where an ancient Chinese man and a young boy attended the needs of the handful of working men who were generally clustered around the counter.

In the center of this virtual treasure trove of a shop stood a booth on a raised platform, its upper part screened in with a slot like a ticket window at the movies. It was here that Seow's customers paid for their purchases, had their sales slip stamped, collected their change. Inside this cage stood Mrs. Seow herself, the lifeblood of the enterprise, constantly shrieking at the various clerks and salesgirls, most of whom were family members.

Entering the store that day I asked a salesgirl where the leatherette was kept. She pointed out a dismal looking display of five or six small rolls in various shades of brown, the largest a particularly hideous mustard color. None of the rolls held more than a few yards, three or four at the most; according to my calculations I needed sixteen yards for each veranda.

"Bring the mauve!" screamed Mrs. Seow. She reminded me of the Red Queen in *Alice in Wonderland*, who ran around shrieking, "Off with their heads!" Presently two salesgirls staggered into view carrying an immense roll of violet colored leatherette. I had no choice.

"Perfect!" "I said. "I'll take thirty two yards."

With a resounding thud the heavy roll was plopped down onto the floor just inside the shop's front door, causing the chamber pots to sway on their wire. As I watched, the two girls unrolled the leatherette straight back through the grocery section, the family kitchen, the family's living quarters, across an alley and onto a rubbish-strewn vacant lot overgrown with weeds. A bull, chewing quietly on his cud, stood tethered on a mound of empty tin cans and broken down cartons. And Lord knows what else.

I picked up some Lysol with which to sanitize my purchase after its exposure to the bull and to the trash strewn yard, as well as a can each of black and white enamel. Then, remembering just in time about the ice pick Vera had asked me to buy, I headed up the hill to Jericho. I sprayed the entire thirty-two yards with Lysol, having with Herman's help, spread the violently violet fabric in the sun. It would probably fade a little in time.

"Mizz Nick, Mizz Nick, you buy de wrong ting!" Vera ran out onto the veranda brandishing the implement I'd dropped off in the kitchen. "Me aks you to buy me one ice PICK!" she exclaimed, bringing her fingers together in a lifting motion.

"Well, if TONGS are called an 'ice pick'," I asked, puzzled, "what do you call this?"

 "An ice prick!" replied Vera.

3 HERMAN

Herman, the gardener we inherited when we bought Jericho had somehow lost an eye earlier on. He looked rather like a pirate, sporting a heavy, black, broad-brimmed fedora shading his good eye; his otherwise bare, brown feet squished around in black, rubber boots; his machete, the universal gardening tool of the area, always at his side.

Herman had other problems besides the loss of an eye; it was paranoia. "People" were always following him around, Herman would tell us, and it was because of the hat. Herman even went so far as to confide to Janney that there were those who thought he was mad!

"But mad people dem stays in Bellevue," Herman reasoned logically, "and me no stay in Bellevue, so me cyaan be mad!" QED.

Sometimes serious gardening problems arose, such as: should the oleander be pruned before or after it blooms, or what should be planted to replace the avocado sapling that the neighbors' goat had eaten?

"How about planting a bed of those pretty little purple flowers?" Janney suggested. "Oh, de penny-wrinkle dem? Me were considrin' dat," Herman replied.

Herman had planted several small fruit trees around the property and some of them were looking a bit droopy. After considerable deliberation, Janney and Herman concluded that a little citrus fertilizer would perk things up. Checking around Ocho Rios, we learned that citrus fertilizer was only available in St. Ann's Bay, the market town of the Parish of St. Ann, known as The Garden Parish, a twenty minute drive west of 'Hochi.' I was elected to go.

The marketplace in St. Ann's Bay is, for all intents and purposes, vertical. It sprawls over a steep slope which reaches down to close-by Discovery Bay where Columbus is said to have moored one or more of his ships in 1494.

Asking several people for directions I finally learned that I was to go to a kiosk of sorts where the administration of the market was located. Once there I spoke to a woman inside a cashier's cage.

"I'm looking to buy some citrus fertilizer," "How much you need?" "What size does it come in?" "You buys it by de pound." "Doesn't it come in a bag?" I asked hopefully. "YOU BUYS IT BY DE POUND;

any amount you want," came the polite but impatient reply. "How much you need?"

"Fifty pounds," I said weakly, hoping they'd at least have a box or bag to put it into. "Seven dollar fifty cent," said the woman. I gave her the money and asked where I was to pick up my purchase.

"In front of the market," she said. She handed me a receipt and busied herself with some paperwork, glad to be finished dealing with such an ignorant foreigner.

Looking around outside the market I saw a few higglers [the word comes from 'hagglers'] selling fruit or vegetables, as well as shoppers carrying bags or baskets. No sign of my fertilizer. Crossing the street I spied a space between two buildings, and there was a young boy raising a hand held scale to his eye level. Reaching down into a large bag that stood at his feet, he carefully added a small scoopful of what I assumed was my fertilizer to a coffee can on the scale, squinted once more at the dial on the scale, leveled off the contents and finally dumped it into a cardboard box. I asked him if that was the way he was going to weigh the entire fifty pounds, and he nodded.

Returning an hour later as he was just finishing up, I saw the very nearly empty bag he'd been scooping from. Printed on its side: '25 kilos'--which translates into 55 pounds.

4 VERA

Vera spoiled me shamelessly, bringing coffee or orange juice to me before breakfast while I lounged by the pool in the early morning sunlight.

Late afternoons we would hear Vera in the kitchen, chipping away with the 'ice prick' I'd mistakenly purchased. She would then emerge as her self-proclaimed 'Auntie Booze Trolley' persona, carrying with her a dreadful concoction made from 180 proof white rum, pineapple juice, lime juice, and a horrid, artificially flavored strawberry syrup.

She also made a liqueur, of sorts, using the same white rum and some of the allspice berries which grew all around; part of the golf course had been an allspice (known locally as pimento) plantation earlier on. The liqueur tasted exactly like Lavoris mouthwash, while the rum, without the additives, tasted and smelled like paint remover and probably had about the same effect on one's innards. When we told Vera we didn't like either of these beverages, she countered, saying, "All de guest-dem love it so! Dem calls de rum punch 'Vera Red Pop!'"

* * * * * * *

After we'd owned Jericho a couple of years, I got a phone call from Vera one day while we were at home in the States. First time renters, friends from Ann Arbor, would soon be staying in Jericho for a couple of weeks.

"Mo-oms, Mo-oms!" (this, not like Mom as in Mommy, was Vera's version of Ma-am). "Herman, 'im gon' mad! 'Im chop de hose ting from de pool wid 'im machete!"

"Well maybe you could ask Mrs. Beaton to get you a roll of duct tape to patch it up and we'll bring a new hose when we come down next month?" I suggested hopefully. "Oh no, mo-oms! Not even one likkl piece remain! You wud no reco'nize it!" she exclaimed.

When our Ann Arbor friends returned from their stay in Jericho, they told us there was a new gardener, Winston. They loved Vera, as I knew they would. Winston, on the other hand seemed to hear voices, or at least to carry on conversations with people who were NOT present. He mimicked the accents, we were told; American, British and Scottish, of various local characters--carrying on both sides of these imagined dialogues.

Winston was a terrible gardener but he was so funny that we kept him on as long as the grounds looked presentable and he kept the pool going. Mrs Beaton borrowed a hose from another property she managed, so everything still kept working until we arrived with the new hose.

WINSTON (WITH BOTTLE CAPS ON EYES) AND GRACE. NOTE WHITE RUM IN FOREGROUND.

The 'staff quarters' at Jericho has three bedrooms besides a kitchen and bath, and stands at the top of the slope across the driveway from the main house. In front is a spacious veranda which catches the cool evening breezes. Soon after we'd gotten to Jamaica that year, we met for the first time Vera's son Bobby, the youngest of her five children, who was staying with her for a while. Daughters Ann and Sharon attended school in Linstead, where they 'boarded' with a woman who lived near the school and they usually came to Upton on weekends. Vera's two older sons were working elsewhere.

Jamaicans love nicknames and almost everyone has one--Vera's family being notable exceptions.

One man has been known as 'Log' ever since he tried to collect insurance on the 'death' of his uncle, the real uncle happily residing in England while his nephew put up a fake tombstone over a log he had buried. Another, known as 'Gas Station,' had driven a truck too tall to fit under the canopy of an ESSO Station, pulling said canopy away.

But our favorite was 'Diamonds!' This woman, a Jamaican of French origin whose name was Mary Isobel, had married a Canadian at the age of eighteen and had lived in Canada for some fifty years when we met her--yet she was known to all as 'Diamonds.' She was the first daughter born into a large family and when her father called her young siblings to see the new baby, he asked, "Could there be anything more precious than a new baby sister?" "Yes! Diamonds!" replied two of her brothers. And the name stuck.

One day, Bobby came down to where I was sitting and said, "Please Miss, canyoutellmewhereispressah?" (Conversations in Jamaica are often fraught with misunderstandings or non-comprehensions.)

"I'm sorry Bobby, I don't understand what you're saying." "Please Miss, canyoutellmewhereispressah?" somewhat louder this time. Vera must have heard. She called down from the veranda, "'Im aks you if you know where is Winston. Us calls 'im 'Presserfoot' 'cuz 'im so knock-knee an' 'im toe-dem looks like de presserfoot on de sewin' machine. Sometime us calls 'im 'Uncle Pressfoot' or jus' plain 'Press.' Bobby call 'im Pressah."

I had also overheard the following conversation between Bobby and Manley, the gardener at Flower Power, the property just below Jericho: "Mr. Manley, Sir, can I borrow your saw, sir?" "Me don't got no saucer, Bobby." "No, sir, Mr. Manley Sir, me aks you if I can borrow your SAW SIR?" "Bobby, me tells you, me don't got no saucer!"

* * * * * * *

One Saturday afternoon at Jericho, I heard the rumble and roar of a motorcycle come into our driveway. "Oh, dat'll be Fudgie," said Vera, "'im com from Kingston an' sells ice cream."

FUDGIE AND JANNEY.

The local version the 'Good Humor' man, all Jamaican mobile ice cream sellers are called Fudgie. This Fudgie's bike had a sidecar half filled with dry ice and containing a small supply of rapidly thawing popsicles, fudgsicles, and something that was new to me ... he held out a 'Nutty Buddy,' called a 'Drumstick' in the US, a small ice cream filled sugar cone, coated with a skim of chocolate, after which the ice cream end was dipped into a handful of chopped peanuts. Vera offered her suggestion, "Fudgie also have stripe ice cream called Napoleon. It have three flavors."

"I'll take four Nutty Buddies," I said, thinking of Vera and Winston as well as of Janney and me.

"Why haven't I ever seen you before?" I asked Fudgie. "When do you come here?" The man thought for a moment before answering, "On Saturday and Sunday I come every day. De res' o de week I come some-times."

We always looked and listened for Fudgie after that, but he came only 'sometimes.'

5 FOX and WILLOW

One day I noticed some little circles of sunlight on the floor at Jericho. The light had to be coming in through the roof, but then, why didn't the rain come in? That was easy; rain had not fallen in some time. We had renters coming the following week and I certainly didn't want it to rain on their parade. The thing to do, Vera said, was to ask Mr. Fox to come and take a look. Vera phoned the office where Mrs. Fox worked and left an urgent message for her husband. We had to see him and we had to see him fast!

A couple of days later a beat up looking jeep pulled into our driveway and out hopped Mr. Fox and his assistant, Maxie (pronounced 'Moxie'). Maxie is a mulatto with crossed blue eyes and wavy yellow hair, usually sporting a hard-hat, set at a rakish angle atop his curls.

Mr. Fox is a middle-aged Bermudian with a speech impediment. His specialty is swimming pool pumps, which he pronounces 'pyumps', making frequent reference to an 'impullah' and something he called a 'blue touch.' We finally figured out that these meant an 'impeller' and a 'blow torch.' Though obviously a leaky roof was not in his area of expertise, Fox, unlike most of the workers in the area, had a vehicle and had access to a telephone in the office his wife worked in: this was the reason why Vera selected him for the job.

Mr. Fox of course said that he could not tell whether or not the roof leaked as it wasn't raining, so Winston was elected to climb up on a ladder and run the hose on the roof while the rest of us kept vigil inside; all that is, except Maxie who was told to climb up into the attic-like crawl space over the kitchen to see if it leaked there. (Only the kitchens and bathrooms of our duplex had dropped ceilings, each living room and bedroom had a high cathedral ceiling with a pair of louvered doors, up high, which opened into these crawl spaces.) Janney, Vera, Mr. Fox and I waited below as the first spatter of water could be heard trickling down the steeply pointed roof. Then, a fairly heavy shower of water from the hose could be heard splashing down outside. Nothing! Not one drop of water appeared in the living room where sunlight had been shining through. At that moment, Winston must have aimed the hose directly over the part of the roof that covered the crawl space, and a terrible yowl (like a cat being run over) issued from above.

The pair of doors to the crawl space burst open and Maxie's head popped out, his blue eyes more crossed than ever, the blond hair sticking our every-which-way. Maxie looked for all the world like a café-au-lait Harpo Marx. Water poured from the brim of his crazily tilted tin hat. We had a cuckoo clock which hung to the side and well below the louvered doors, and at that very moment the smaller, cuckoo clock doors opened up and the small carved wooden bird popped out. "Cuckoo, cuckoo, cuckoo!" We were all doubled over with laughter; all but Maxie that is, who thought we were laughing at him. Understandably, he was furious. "Me not goin' up dere nex' time!' he announced, shaking the water from his head.

Of course neither Janney nor I knew that Mr. Fox suffered from fear of heights, so clearly he would not be the one to climb up and repair the roof. Now it appeared that neither would Maxie.

Vera then came up with another brilliant idea, "We must call for Mr. Willow!" Mr. Fox nodded vigorously while Maxie just continued to drip.

The gentleman in question is a carpenter whose real name is Ansel Wilmot, Wilmot being the surname of around one third of the population of the small town of Lodge, situated about 2 1/2 miles up the hill from

Upton. Like most of his neighbors, Willow, as he is known to all, has neither a vehicle nor a phone. Vera called Mrs. Edwards whose small grocery store is not quite a mile away, asking her to take down a message for Willow, should he happen to pop in.

We caught our first glimpse of Mr. Willow as he ambled down our driveway carrying a saw. "Me knows Miss Vera have a hammer," he said, smiling as he jingled a few nails in his pocket. He climbed the ladder which was still in place, and after a brief inspection of the work site, announced rather apologetically, that he'd have to charge fifty dollars to repair the roof, which at the exchange rate of the day was about nineteen dollars in US money. I had a new, instant hero!

Not a man to waste words, Mr. Willow asked Vera if she had any old tins. Vera brought out some empty paint cans from under a shrub and Willow got to work. Pulling tin shears from his pocket he quickly cut open the cans and using Vera's hammer, flattened them before returning to the roof. We could hear him walking around and hammering away up there, removing an occasional shingle, and nailing down part of a tin can before replacing the shingle. More walking--more hammering. The hammering went on for quite a long time before a neighbor who happened to be passing by, said that he'd seen Willow up on the roof waving his arms frantically. Wind had blown the ladder down and Willow had been hammering to attract our attention, having long since finished the work. The situation was quickly remedied and a visibly shaken Mr. Willow climbed carefully down from the roof. Janney gave the poor man a beer and a shot of rum to calm his nerves.

*   *   *   *   *   *   *

Years later, after we'd sold Jericho and moved into a nearby condominium, we thought of Mr. Willow when our screens needed some work. Willow arrived, older, but with the same loose-jointed shuffle, again carrying his saw. But this time our neighbors' dog 'Lady' ran up to him snarling and baring her teeth. Willow was obviously frightened. Janney called off the dog and escorted the old man to our door. The poor soul was visibly distressed but at the same time somewhat embarrassed at being cowardly. He said he had known the dog for years and had, in fact. "taken care a 'im when a car mash 'im op." (Gender means nothing in Jamaican speech.)

"Dog ungrateful!" he said. "Me take care a 'im when ee were constipated fe twenty eight day!" But after a cigarette and a few calming sips of beer, Willow began to think better of it.

"Maybe 'im not know me in me new glasses," he suggested. Mr. Willow worries a lot about getting 'sugar' (diabetes) from a dog bite.

"Dog 'ave ninety-nine germ in 'im mout, y' know! Dog not brush 'im teeth, y' know!" he added. Then, with a shy smile and a twinkle in his eye, Mr. Willow polished off his beer and got to work on our screens.

6 The CRUSTY CURMUDGEON

I've heard of lovable old curmudgeons and irascible or crusty curmudgeons, never any young curmudgeons, loveable or otherwise. P. K. Saunders falls into both the 'old' and the 'irascible' categories.

We first met P.K. back in the days when he and his wife Barbara still owned the Upton Golf Course [now Sandals] and were spending their winters in Jamaica, living in their apartment over the course's clubhouse. The house was painted pink and had been built in the style of an old plantation home, or 'Great House' as they are called in Jamaica. The couple spent their summers in Connecticut and eventually moved to Manteo, North Carolina. Saunders had designed and built the Upton Golf Course, and he and Barbara, who was his third wife, would play a round in the late afternoon each day when they were on the island. In this pleasant way they were able to oversee the maintenance of their property.

During our yearly vacation trips to Jamaica we would see the Saunders riding around Upton or Ocho Rios in their red jeep, its canvas roof folded back. Barbara (who is a sensible English woman) did the driving, while P.K., wearing a pith helmet, looked totally oblivious to everything except what he was talking about, and he was always talking. A large man, he seemed to stare above the heads of mere mortals, his pointed grey beard jutting out arrogantly.

I was mildly surprised when at a cocktail party Barbara introduced Janney and me to her husband. I hadn't thought she knew we existed.

"It's the Nichols, Phil!" "Harrumph." "They've bought Jericho from the Eustaces." "Harrumph."

I was even more surprised when she invited us to play golf with them the following afternoon.

After that Janney and I would join them from time to time; the three of them played, P.K. talked, and I walked around and listened. It certainly wasn't much of a workout walking around with them as P.K. would stop every time he hit the ball and tell one of his stories.

He had written his own modern version of the Bible, calling it the 'Space-Age Jehovah.' In his rendering, the people of Great Britain had been one of the lost tribes of Israel; the name 'Britain' having come from a corruption of the term 'Brithain', as in 'B'nai Brith'. (A Jewish organization, whose name translates as 'Children of the Covenant.') Adam and Eve, it seems, were not the first man and woman on Earth, they were merely the first of a 'superior brand' to have come to Earth from outer space. 'Aborigines' already inhabited our planet when Adam and Eve descended, we are told by P.K., and it was from among these 'aborigines' that Cain chose his wife.

Saunders had also written his autobiography, which, along with 'The Space-Age Jehovah,' he had kindly loaned to us. In it he tells of his birth in South Africa, his early childhood in England, his having been sent to boarding school at the age of three and of holidays during which he and his sister would run around the house squirting each other with seltzer bottles. At the age of five, P.K. tells us, he joined the Royal Navy and went to sea.

In the autobiography as well as during his conversations (and I use the word conversation loosely; P.K. always had his hearing aid unplugged and was simply oblivious to another person's attempts at speaking), he refers to his various wives as: numbers 'One', 'Two' or 'Three.' He does, however address Barbara as 'Ba-ah' when speaking to her. He has one child, Margaret, from one of the earlier marriages.

P.K. goes on to describe his invention of the Saunders Valve which many years earlier had become a state-of-the-art component of dairy milking machines and was still widely in use at the time, earning him a substantial income and freedom, as there was no need for him to hold down a job. He acquired a yacht in which he, along with whichever wife was current, would sail the Caribbean, stopping in the Bahamas from time to time to play golf with the Prince of Wales (later the Duke of Windsor), when he was in residence there. The Prince liked to win, we were told, and it was deemed 'politically correct' for those who moved in such circles to indulge him in this way.

Stopping in Jamaica on one of his voyages, P.K. recognized the enormous potential of an area of rolling hills called Upton, just a few miles southeast of Ocho Rios. There he bought a property which included a neglected allspice plantation as well as a citrus grove on which the golf course now stands.

When P.K. designed the course he located the first tee on a small hill, some thirty feet above the rest of the course. Golfers rode from the clubhouse to the tee in a picturesque cart, driven by

VERA AND HER BROTHERS.

Vera's brother Harold, drawn by a mule named 'Diamond.' This added a lot of charm to an already breathtakingly beautiful view with the blue Caribbean to the north.

Years later, P.K. sold the golf course to John Collier, an Englishman who had been his long-time manager. Now retired and living in Manteo, P.K. and Ba-ah would sometimes spend a week or ten days as our guests at Jericho.

There were advantages to having an irascible curmudgeon as a houseguest; we didn't have to worry about entertaining him or any other guests we might happen to have. The curmudgeon would do it all himself--just by being outrageous.

P.K. frequently prefaced his remarks, saying: "All Americans/Canadians/Jamaicans, etc., are of course incredibly stupid ... " depending on whether the person he was talking to was an American, a Canadian or a Jamaican. One time when friends from Ann Arbor, Abby and Sam Conners, were also visiting, P.K. went into his "All Americans are incredibly stupid" routine, stating that what we all think of as Ann Arbor, of course is really 'Anne's Harbour'. Abby tried to persuade him otherwise, but eventually, almost in tears, she realized her words were literally falling on 'deaf ears;' the hearing aid of course was unplugged. We from Ann Arbor knew otherwise. We had all heard the story of its naming for the wives of two original settlers: Ann Allen and Mary Ann Rumsey in a grove of burr oak in the then dense woods of the Michigan Territory. It was originally named Annarbor.

The Saunders were extremely close with the dollar, especially considering that we all knew they had sold the golf course for a million dollars, still a substantial amount at that time. Ba-ah normally wore old trousers, topped by an old tee shirt of P.K.'s, well washed but sometimes with unmistakable traces of old paint stains. It was even rumored that the caddies had taken up a collection to buy her a dress, but this had evidently not materialized; she continued to wear the same old outfits.

On one notable occasion, we were hosting a party to welcome a long absent resident; Upton's own Lady Diana. A Dutch woman by birth, the 'Ladyship' was conferred on Diana for her work aiding downed RAF pilots in Holland during World War II.

She owned a beautiful home, Monticello, atop Upton's highest

LADY DIANA'S HOME, MONTICELLO

hilltop. An elderly woman, she and her American husband who was some years her junior, spent most of their time in Lausanne, Switzerland, coming to Jamaica from time to time.

Ba-ah was apparently so impressed with the importance of the guest of honor that she wore a skirt that was obviously of her own creation. She had purchased a yard and a half or so of black cotton fabric, gathered the top onto an elastic waistband and had partially sewn up one side leaving a slit for maneuverability. But alas, this slit was not enough. Ba-ah had been standing by our pool looking down at the golf course when she heard voices from the house. She turned and on seeing Diana on the verandah, attempted a full curtsey but was hobbled by the skirt and very nearly fell into the pool. I pretended not to notice.

On another occasion, during an evening party on our verandah, P.K. suddenly rose to his feet to illustrate a point in the story he was telling. In so doing, he accidentally banged his head sharply into a heavy wrought-iron chandelier that hung from a chain, normally over a table; but P.K. had moved the table out of his way. The chandelier's eight candles, still aflame, flew in all directions, one of them landing in the lap of a guest, Mrs. Redman, who was wearing a nylon dress. It was fortunate the chandelier did not have glass chimneys. It continued to sway ominously on its creaking chain while everyone except 'Number Three' hovered anxiously around P.K., feeling his head and asking his how he felt. He, on the other hand, continued his story without missing a beat while quick thinking Ba-ah dumped her drink into the lap of the smoldering dress and was furiously stamping out the still burning candles. The nylon dress was ruined but Mrs. Redman remained unscathed. I found an apron for her to wear for the rest of the evening over the gaping hole in her dress.

The following morning John Collier stopped by as Janney and I along with our four houseguests were seated on the verandah enjoying a second cup of the delicious Blue Mountain coffee for which Jamaica is so justly famous. "Letter for you, Phil," John said with a smile. Vera brought him a cup of coffee and he pulled up a chair while extending an envelope to P.K.

P.K. harrumphed a couple of times and read the letter aloud. It began; "Dear Dad." The writer went on to explain that his mother had been a certain 'Mavis Green', whom he was quite certain 'Dad' would re-member. The letter went on to speak of financial matters and plans for school. It was signed, 'Michael Saunders.'

P.K., not even slightly nonplused, remarked, "Ba-ah, I didn't have SEK-sual intercourse with Mavis Green, did I?" "Eow! I don't believe so, Phil," replied 'Number Three,' calmly. "Besides," added P.K.,

"Mavis was Chinese, so her name wouldn't be Green, it would be Wong or Fong or something like that!"

As P.K. returned the letter to its envelope, a small photograph dropped to the table.

We glimpsed a young, tannish face, surrounded by a huge halo of black hair. "Always have despised these blasted afro hairdos!" Placing it and the letter in his shirt pocket, he continued to sip his coffee. No further mention was made of the incident.

7 PEACOCKS

Back in the days when Janney and I were both still working for the University, we were able to spend at most four or five weeks a year in Jamaica. From time to time while back home in Ann Arbor we would receive a phone call from Mrs. Beaton, the elderly Scottish woman we were fortunate to have looking after Jericho when we weren't there. When she called, it usually was to tell us to send more money, or to ask if we'd accept a 'long term,' or a 'local' rental in the off-season. This generally referred to the manager of a bank or a hotel, who had been transferred to the area and needed a place to stay while looking for a house; or it might be someone who would be working in Ocho Rios on a temporary basis. We would always agree if we didn't have any other rentals coming up since the income from a 'local' rental, though much lower than an in-season or tourist rental still brought in some very welcome cash and would USUALLY not require any additional expenses on our part. Local renters paid their own utilities while we continued to pay Vera and the gardener.

However, not all of Mrs. Beaton's local rentals could be termed a success; in fact there were a couple that could be termed complete disasters! A young man, Michael, whom Mrs. B had known 'in his woolies' (which I assume meant baby clothes), wished to rent one half of Jericho for the summer. He and his girl-friend Veronica moved in and a few days later a group of American kids contacted Mrs. B, wanting to rent the other half of the duplex. If Mrs. B had no prob-lem with this, it was fine with us.

* * * * * * *

Michael was in the process of inventing a 'perpetual motion' machine. He was under water in the deep end of the pool fiddling with his contraption which was sending great plumes of water high up into the air when the American youngsters arrived. The two girls quickly changed into their bikinis and had just come down to the pool to catch a few rays when suddenly the 'perpetual' motion stopped being perpetual; it had stopped spewing. Michael, who was without benefit of a swimsuit, arose from the depths, cursing a blue streak. The two girls screamed and ran into their half of the house. Michael ran behind them, not as the girls supposed to chase them but to enter his half of the house and call Mrs. B to complain that the new-comers had interfered with his invention.

One of the girls shamelessly phoned her mother, saying she'd been in an accident and needed more money. This having been done, the girls moved into a hotel, while Michael and Veronica found an arrangement similar to Jericho in Turks and Caicos, a group of islands close to the Bahamas

* * * * * * *

On another occasion, Mrs. B spoke to us of a lovely English girl, Deirdre, who had come to Jamaica to recover from a broken heart. She wanted to rent just a quarter of Jericho, one bedroom and bath, that is, for the summer. There were no rentals coming up, so we agreed and thought no more of it.

Around mid-August of that year, while in Ann Arbor, we received a call from a man, a Jamaican, who said he had a buyer for Jericho. We were definitely interested; rentals were not going well, partly due to Socialist tendencies on the part of the Prime Minister, Michael Manley, who was developing close ties with Fidel Castro. We also felt that a smaller place would be more to our liking and there was a condo in the same neighborhood that would soon become available. Both of us would be retiring before too long. It would be good to get out of the rental business and spend more time in Jamaica.

I phoned Vera asking her to make sure Jericho would be ready to be shown early in September.

"Oh Mo-oms!" she sobbed. "You mus' come down here! Sometin' turrble goin' on!" She was crying so hard I could scarcely understand what she was saying.

Janney couldn't get away just then and I was about to start a new project on my job a couple of weeks later, so I was elected to go to Jamaica, and hopefully to solve whatever the problem was, as well as to be there when the potential buyers came to look at the house. A day later all the necessary arrangements had been made and I flew down. All sorts of horrible scenarios passed through my mind, but I couldn't possibly guess what had actually taken place.

Our lovely young English tenant, Deirdre, had recovered from her broken heart in rather short order, quickly finding a new, live-in love--a 'Rasta.' A Rasta(farian) is a member of the Rastafarian move-ment which originated in Jamaica and which considers the late Haile Selassie to be God. A true Rastafarian does not eat pork and does not cut his hair or beard; he does however smoke marijuana (ganja or 'the gange') as a religious rite. I can't recall whether or not they drink rum.

There are quite a few young Jamaican men who

pretend to be Rastas; grow their hair and beard and wear Rasta-type colorful clothing, because they hope to maybe catch a rich girl 'who come from foreign.' And often they do manage to pick up an American or Canadian lass they can move in with and live off of for a few weeks or a few months, or until the girl runs out of money or has to return to her job or her parents.

I don't know which kind of Rasta, Deirdre's friend 'Innocence' was, but I suspect he was of the latter sort, known to some as a 'Rent-a-Rasta.'

Innocence invited a pair of his friends, a French couple, to join him and Deirdre in Jericho. The couple; Jean-Claude and Monique, apparently led a double life: they 'made movies' by day and engaged in the 'ganja' trade by night. To make matters worse, they enlisted the aid of Winston (Presserfoot), the gardener, in their nefarious pursuits. He worked for them all night long packaging the weed and helping them load it onto trucks or whatever other vehicles they could commandeer for the purpose. In return they gave him a radio and other electronic devices.

By day, the ganja was stored in the crawl space high up above Jericho's kitchens, in the very same place where the water had poured down on poor Maxie's head. There was evidence that our 'tenants' had put the metal stair step stool on top of the buffet and pulled themselves up and into the small opening with the louvered doors. Their footprints were visible on the wall below.

* * * * * *

When I got there it was also clear that Winston's nighttime activities had taken their toll. The garden and grounds had been totally neglected, but fortunately the pool was still in good shape, most likely because our 'tenants' wanted to enjoy its use. When Winston heard that I was on my way he pulled up all the plants that had died or were in the process of dying, and on the day of my arrival he stuck begonias into the holes in the ground where the plants had been. The whole crowd had dispersed; Vera and Winston were there to greet me and tell me the tale of woe.

Though curious, I thought it best to maintain some 'gravitas' and not to ask Vera about the exact nature of the movies that Jean-Claude and Monique had been making, but when I told her I was going to town to buy paint, she said, "Oh no, Mo-oms, lots o' paint stay from de movies--dem use it fe' blood." When I replied that I needed it to repaint the wall with the footprints, she said "De paint, it white." Winston, hoping to atone, said he knew where he could borrow a couple of paintbrushes.

The morning after my arrival found me at the hardware store buying sandpaper and varnish to repair the buffet top and pigment to make the 'blood paint'

45

match the wall color.

Vera then told me, "De drain dem plog op an' de septic tank overflow!" It seems Mrs. Beaton had been called away and a young woman, Jeanne Dixon, had taken her place. Vera had called Jeanne repeatedly about the septic tank, "but 'im no listen." Vera had then called a plumber who said the 'clog' was much further down the line than he could reach. Neither Vera nor the plumber could find anyone who knew the exact location of the septic tank, much less the 'clog.' It turned out that Deirdre had been trimming Innocence's hair and beard (this proved he was not a true Rasta), and it was this hair that was clogging up the plumbing.

That afternoon, Vera and I left Winston painting out the footprints on the wall and we drove around from one construction site to another looking for someone we could 'pirate,' who would dig up the yard and find the drain, but to no avail. Presently Vera remembered that one of her church sisters had a son, Donny, who did sewer work for one of the hotels, but she didn't know which of the hotels he worked in. We drove around some more and Vera asked her numerous church brethren and 'sistern' whom we encountered along the way, "Do you know where Donny muddah live?"

Finally, with Vera navigating, we pulled up at the foot

of a very steep bluff and Vera bounded up like a gazelle. Having gotten the needed information she returned a few minutes later and told me that we must go to the San Susie ('Sans Souci'), a lovely old resort hotel a few miles up the coast.

After a lot of inquiries we located Donny, and Vera spoke to him in the kind of Jamaican Patois that I don't understand. Donny replied similarly and walked away. Vera and I strolled around the hotel grounds for a bit and then returned to the car which I had left parked in the shade under a tree. After about forty-five minutes of waiting I finally asked, "Vera, where is Donny? What are we doing here? When is Donny coming back?"

"'Im gon look for 'im peacocks. 'im friend 'ave de key fe 'im lockah," Vera replied in a matter of fact sort of way. This sounded interesting, but how were PEA-COCKS going to fix our drain? At last Donny appeared carrying a large pickaxe (peek-ocks to my untrained ear). Donny and his 'peacocks' got into the car and away we went, back up the hill to our clogged drain.

After a lot of digging, Donny located the septic tank which to my untrained eye looked kind of small for a house the size of Jericho; but what do I know? Donny dug up some more dirt all around the tank. After taking him back to the Sans Souci, Vera and I went shopping.

Along the way, Vera spotted a friend. She called, "Yo, Yunik!" Surprised, I exclaimed, "Vera, what are you saying?" She replied, "Oh, us calls 'im Unicorn."

We bought as many cinder blocks as the trunk of the rental car could hold, and after loading a bag of cement onto the back seat we headed up the hill; past the entrance to Upton, past the village of Lodge, all the way to the top, to a place called Cascade, where a

VERA SUPERVISES DONNY'S REPAIRS TO THE SEPTIC TANK.

huge wooden pipe carries water from a reservoir to the surrounding area. A large sign there bore the message: 'Do Not Remove River Sand!'

Once again I was puzzled as Vera unloaded a shovel and a thick paper cement

JANNEY, VERA, AND DRIVER IN FRONT OF THE HUGE WOODEN WATER DELIVERY PIPE

bag that I hadn't noticed before. "Com-on Mo-oms, us gonna dig. Dis river sand doan got salt like de beach sand." Vera saw me looking at the sign, "Iss okay, Mo-oms, me son David work up here; juss hold de bag open so I cyan put in de sand."

Three days later I picked up Jericho's potential buyers at their hotel and proudly drove them up the hill to see Jericho; a Jericho gleaming with fresh paint and varnish, with newly planted shrubs and flowers growing where the old ones had died, and a newly enlarged septic tank with unclogged drains, thanks to Donny and 'im peacocks!

The potential buyers fell in love Jericho; they made an offer. I accepted and we made plans to close in December.

8 MR SEVENS

As soon as the deal on Jericho was made we quickly

JANNEY CONTEMPLATES
POST-RETIREMENT CAREER
OPTIONS--GOATHERD?

bought the apartment, a condominium actually, that we'd had our eye on for some time. The 'condo' is right there in the same area as Jericho, same view, same neighbors, very close as the crow flies, but about a five-minute walk on the winding road.

Closing day on Jericho was still a month away when we made an early trip to Jamaica to move our personal things from Jericho and prepare our new place for habitation. On arrival we were greeted by Vera, excitedly telling me, "Mo-oms, Mo-oms, us has a new gyardener! An' 'im a cyarpenter! Mrs. Beaton come back an' her fire Presserfoot! 'Im a caddie now," Vera told us.

"A carpenter, huh? " Janney said, "Good, we'll put him to work building shelves in the new apartment. What's his name?"

"Well", said Vera, "'im name sumpin' like 'Yardman Eleven', but eleven too big a number for so likkl a mon, so dem calls 'im 'Sebbens' [Sevens]."

And as we could see for ourselves when he arrived the next morning, he was indeed small, maybe five foot two and he bore an uncanny resemblance to Redd Foxx of junkyard fame.

"Yaroman Treleven is me name Mr. Nick an' Mizz. Nick," our new employee introduced himself. And the junkyard connection persisted when we saw an example of his 'cyarpentry;' a cabinetmaker he was not. In retrospect, though, it was a pretty good example of ingenuity--of what you CAN do, even if you have nothing. Mr. Sevens had taken a wheel from an abandoned lawn mower and a few old boards and constructed himself a wheelbarrow with discarded broom-sticks as handles.

At first, Sevens used to come to Jericho each morning carrying what he thought he would need for the day in a large box which he balanced on his head. The box looked almost bigger than he did. Later on he found it easier just to stay at Jericho. He created a sort of lean-to arrangement where he maintained a troll-like existence between two of the pillars supporting the pool terrace on the steep slope down to the golf course.

* * * * * * *

One day Mr. Sevens was going to the shop, a small grocery store less than a mile away, to buy something for his lunch. Vera asked him to get her a nutmeg, planning to make rum punch for us. I gave the little man a dollar (worth about 38 US cents at that time) and thought no more of it. Sometime later I heard a tremendous ruckus in the kitchen; then Vera came running out to the veranda. "Mo-oms! Mo-oms! How much money you gib to Sebbens?" "A dollar," I replied.

"Mo-oms! 'Im only bring back fifteen cent!" Vera ran to the phone and called Mrs. Edwards at the shop. "Mizz E, fe' how much you sell nutmeg? Forty five cent?" shrieked Vera. "Sebbens jus' bring back fifteen cent change fe' Mizz Nick!" Ashamed as I was of my weakness in not interceding for the pathetic little man, I had long ago learned not to interfere in this type of thing! If I were to say to just forget it, the result would be Sevens and me pitted against these two strong women: Vera and Mrs. Edwards. Decidedly a losing proposition! Nor could I undermine Vera's authority in the matter. We'd be moving out soon, leaving Vera running the place for the new owners.

Vera now confronted Sevens directly, "What you do wi' di res' o Mizz Nick change?" Sevens sort of scuffed his foot around and without looking at Vera mumbled that he had bought two nutmegs--and lost one. "You do no soch ting! You tief Mizz Nick forty cent!"

* * * * * * *

I must pause now to explain about Mrs. Edwards' shop; this was no ordinary grocery store. It was a grocery store AND a bar besides being a butcher shop--its actual name was 'Economic Meat Processors.' It also was the communications center for the entire area and Mrs. E was the nerve center of it all. Though of course she'd never heard the term 'multi-tasking' she WAS able to do four things at once, and was frequently called upon to do so. It was not at all unusual to see her checking in a delivery of groceries as boxes were unloaded from a truck, ringing up a sale on the cash register for a customer in the store, taking an order on the telephone, all the while yelling orders to her husband and two sons who were noisily sawing up huge, unrecognizable slabs of frozen beef in the back of the shop.

In a place where most people didn't have a phone or a vehicle, local folk could leave or collect messages with Mrs. E. She knew who was working and who wasn't. Who was drunk, who was broke, who was in trouble.

And Mr. Sevens was in trouble; big trouble, at home, at Jericho and at Mrs. E's grocery store! Sevens would normally have his paycheck cashed by Mrs. E, who would hold out a portion of his pay for Sevens' little grandson, who would come to collect it to take home to the family. Meanwhile, Sevens would be getting drunk at the bar.

MR SEVENS IN THE GARDEN.

After the nutmeg episode however, Sevens was afraid to go to the store. He didn't cash his paycheck that week and spent all his spare time sleeping in his 'house' under our pool. By the time the following week's paycheck came, the little man was desperate. On Friday, he finally screwed up his courage and went to the store to cash both checks. He then proceeded to get drunk! Wondrously drunk! DRUNK! DRUNK! DRUNK!

Sevens was so drunk he wasn't even aware when Mr.

E. and his sons tied him to the grillwork on the window behind the barstool Sevens' was sitting on; perhaps an act of kindness so that he wouldn't fall off the stool when they closed up for the night.

The next morning, when the little grandson (whom a houseguest of ours, an engineer, had dubbed: Mr. One-Point-Seven-Five, reasoning that Sevens' son would be 'Three-and-a-Half') came to collect the household money, he found Sevens still passed out-- still tied to the grillwork. The youngster ran home crying.

Someone finally cut Sevens loose, put him into a pickup truck and unceremoniously dumped him into his 'house,' where he slept for two days and two nights without even moving. He then disappeared, coming back only to retrieve his meager belongings and to tell Vera that he was going to sue Mr. Nick for firing him without notice.

"Stop you foolishness!" Vera told him. "'Im no fire you--you walk off de job!"

When we last heard, Sevens was working for a Canadian dynamiter.

9 EXCHANGE

No one knows why the village, which rambles down a two-and-a-half mile stretch of narrow road is named Exchange (or 'Hexchange,' as pronounced by the local populace). The road follows, roughly, the course of the White River which meanders down the hill from the Cascade reservoir, entering the sea just east of the Shaw Park Beach Hotel.

Among the houses and the few stores and bars scattered along the way, several churches and three or four schools are tucked in here and there, some with their stand-pipes and privies visible from the road.

There is no public transportation in the area other than the privately owned taxis known as 'robots', which collect as many passengers as they can hold before careening down the curving road. But mostly people are on foot. No matter what the hour, school children can always be seen walking up or down the road, the girls wearing white or pink blouses under starched navy blue jumpers, the boys in freshly pressed khakis. Some mornings, coming down a path from be-

IN FRONT OF ECONOMIC MEAT PROCESSORS.

hind the Pepto Bismol colored 'Economic Meat Processors,' you might see a middle-aged man, nattily dressed in a tailored suit and carrying an attaché case, making his way down the hill astride a mule.

Farther down the hill you might see Roggy or Enos, two of life's unfortunates who have not been dealt a full deck. Enos just walks up and down the road while Roggy heads for the hotels along the coast in hopes that some tourist will buy him a shot of rum; sometimes more than one.

A story is told about the day Roggy had a little too much rum and became disorderly. A policeman who happened to be in the bar at the time cautioned Roggy to behave himself; Roggy kicked him. The policeman had no choice but to arrest Roggy on a 'drunk and disorderly' charge. When the case came before the court, everyone from the area who could possibly fit in was in the crowded courtroom.

The judge, who in Jamaica as in England, still wears a white wig while he is speaking, raps his gavel and orders the excited crowd to be quiet. The atmosphere is stifling; there is no air conditioning in the ancient building. A lazy fan wafts the sultry air slowly about. The judge removes the wig and fans himself with it when not actually speaking; replacing the wig when the need to speak once more arises.

"Ragland T. Scott," intones the judge, "is it true that you kicked an officer of the law while he was performing his sworn duty?" "Yessir!" replies Roggy. "Kick 'im in de shin, I did; kick 'im right in de shin!" Nervous titters turn to irrepressible laughter. "Order in the court," raps the judge, removing the wig and mopping his mahogany brow.

"Gin and tonic," responds Roggy. Total bedlam ensues. Unable to control the crowd, the judge, once more placing the wig on his head, dismisses Roggy with as much dignity as he can muster. Since then, people riding up or down the hill in the 'robots' always shout, "Gin and Tonic" when they see Roggy. He just laughs happily.

Although there is nothing the least bit touristy about

Exchange itself, side roads leading east to the White River (which actually looks milky gray) display signs advertising 'River Attractions;' small open air bars, gift shops and perches where the intrepid can dive from a very high bank into a relatively deep river pool. Evenings, locals as well as tourists can enjoy 'A Night on the White River,' a torch-lit cruise on a bamboo raft, poled gondola style and ending with dinner, dancing and reggae music, all against the backdrop of flickering torchlight.

10 HECTOR DUNCAN

We met Hector Duncan on our second trip to Jamaica when he picked us up at the airport; a driver from Sunshine Auto Rentals, an Ocho Rios agency from which we would be renting a car during our two week stay. We had plenty to do; we'd bought Jericho the day before returning to Ann Arbor after our first trip to Jamaica and had really barely taken in all there was to see (and what needed to get done!).

Duncan's job was to transport to or from the airport, the visitors who would then pick up their rental car at the agency or find it parked in the driveway of the place they were renting. We always asked for driver Duncan on our yearly visits even though it was clear that he sometimes enjoyed a libation; he was an excellent driver. Poor Duncan, however, had a lot of problems. For one thing, he had an ulcer (which he called his 'holster'), and he had lost most of his teeth; only one very large tooth was visible in the front of Duncan's ravaged mouth. What with these two conditions, he was reduced to a diet of Horlicks' Malted Milk, and 'creamie,' whatever that might be. When people asked him how he was doing, he'd cheerfully reply, "Still jus' 'avin' Orlicks an' creamie." This new-found sobriety, however, unfortunately, was not destined to last.

Duncan was really troubled by his lack of teeth. He finally persuaded his employers, the Dixons, to advance him enough of his salary to have a set of dentures made. On receiving the money, he went immediately to the racetrack and lost every penny betting on the horses. Two years passed. This time Duncan asked his employers to hold money out of his pay so that he could buy himself some teeth. At last, he had accumulated enough to have his plates made. The employers gave the money directly to Dr. Ffolkes, so there would be no slip up this time. BUT on the night before Duncan was scheduled to pick up the completed dentures, Dr. Ffolkes' office burned to the ground. No insurance! Duncan, still with just the one tooth was still 'jus 'avin' Orlicks and creamie.' But that's not really true. Duncan was consuming large amounts of the Jamaican white rum that is 180 proof. We'd had an opened bottle of it at our place for a long time--it had lost its cork, so we improvised a bottle cap out of aluminum foil. The FUMES actually ate a hole through the lid. No wonder Duncan had a 'holster!'

Duncan was quite a scamp. On one occasion, I was going to Montego Bay alone; that is, without Janney. Duncan was driving me to pick up a guest at the airport. Appearing to be much concerned for my comfort and well-being during our drive there, he asked, "It is very 'ot, Miz Nick. It is still very early, 'ow about us stop so you can 'ave a cool drink?" "Okay," I said. "Let's stop." It WAS hot and we WERE plenty early. He pulled off the road in front of a seedy, rundown looking bar. I went in and ordered a 'Ting,' a delicious grapefruit flavored soft drink, and before I knew it I heard Duncan order a 'gin and wine.'

"Dunkie!" I exclaimed, "What about your ulcer?" Every man in that bar (and they were all men there) burst out laughing. I'd been set up!

It was too late. He'd already downed the revolting concoction and was about to order another when I walked out of the bar and got into the car, swearing I would never ride with Hector Duncan again.

But then there was my birthday. Our daughter, Kathy was on the island staying with friends near Oracabessa. We decided to have dinner at Moxon's near Boscobel, a lovely restaurant located halfway down a seaside precipice, on an overhanging ledge that reached out over the sea. Oliver Moxon, its owner, was a suave Englishman who was actually a member of the Parrish Council and was active in community enterprises.

A MUCH-EXPANDED MOXON'S BEACH CLUB, IN 2013.

On the evening of my birthday, with Duncan driving, we would pick up Kathy and proceed to Moxons, where we would eat a gourmet meal amid breathlessly beautiful surroundings--enjoy a few drinks and know we would be driven to our respective homes in safety.

Janney, Kathy, and I, having been greeted by the jovial Mr. M., were ordering our drinks when Hector Duncan sauntered up to our table, picked up an empty chair from a neighboring table, and turning it around, straddled the seat grinning impishly as he peered at us over the back while snapping his fingers to catch the waiter. Kathy gazed at us imploringly--obviously concerned that this would stir up a ruckus, but the suave Moxon came to the rescue of all of us, and addressed Duncan, "Give the Gov'ner a break, Mate, I'll fix you up over here," as he led him to the bar.

He must have given him a very weak one followed by

plenty of coffee. A very sober Hector Duncan drove us all to our homes and there we said 'goodbye' to him forever.

On another occasion, we had visitors from Ann Arbor, Frank and Lil, who wanted to take us out to dinner, and Janney suggested Moxon's, but this time without the services of Mr. Duncan. Moxon employs an ancient man, possibly a retired waiter, who greets people on their arrival, helping them from the car and then leading them to the steep, rock hewn staircase from the parking lot to the restaurant some fifty feet below.

Our friends had recently married after years of living together while waiting for one of their divorces or the other to come through. When the elderly man handed Lil from the car, he greeted her with the traditional Jamaican word term for 'Missus,' which in the lingo of the land comes out as 'Mistress' with the upward lilt that makes it sound like a question. "No!" stormed Lil. "We were married three months ago!" I am only thankful her husband, a linguist, didn't hear her. He would never have stopped teasing her.

II. Out of Many, One People

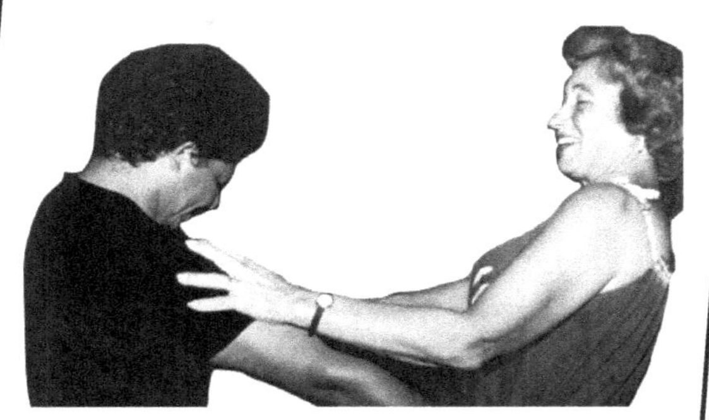

11 OUT of MANY, ONE PEOPLE

Jamaica's motto could not be more appropriate! The island has been a real melting pot since 1494 when Christopher Columbus and his men first made landfall on Jamaica's north coast. The peaceful Arawak Indians they encountered were quickly annihilated by early Spanish settlers who enslaved them, worked them to death or killed them with the diseases they had brought with them to the New World.

ARAWAK DANCERS, AS PORTRAYED BY EARLY EUROPEANS.

In order to escape the Spanish Inquisition, many Sephardic Jews migrated to the island from the Iberian Peninsula; from Portugal as well as from Spain. With the arrival of the British in 1655 and their troops' subsequent victory over the Spanish five years later, many of the Spaniards departed leaving behind only their Spanish place-names, while large numbers of those descended from the Portuguese settlers, remained.

One sees Portuguese family names everywhere, particularly on thriving businesses in the cities. During one of our stays in Jamaica, I noticed that the Rabbi of the Kingston Synagogue and the Bishop of Kingston bore the same Portuguese surname: De Souza. Others came from Syria and Lebanon in much smaller numbers, but are still noticeable, especially in the dry goods, clothing, and hospitality businesses.

The African slave trade, which began in 1507, flourished until 1838, at which time emancipation became the law throughout the British Empire. Vast sugar plantations began to founder due to the shortage of labor and indentured servitude began. People who came from India as well as from China had been sold into another form of slavery, just as brutal; this however was for a specific length of time. When their term expired the workers were free to go, to create new lives for themselves. Many chose to remain in Jamaica, and as we can see, many prospered.

Today's Jamaicans come in all sizes, shapes and colors. I know two Jamaican women who are as fair and blond as any English lass, as well as a married couple who refer to themselves as 'Red Jamaicans;' perhaps their heritage includes Irish or German ancestors. The various sources I've consulted in which demographic statistics appear [*The World Book Almanac* and *Wikipedia*], pretty much agree that the population of the island is 90% Black and 6% 'mixed;' the remainder comprised mainly of people with East Indian, Chinese, Middle Eastern or European backgrounds. Certainly most of the people I see are almost all Black, but in their dark faces one occasionally spies blue or grey eyes, or Asian features, or a certain look which undeniably originated in India. My question is: who is it that comprises the 6% 'mixed' population? My guess is that many more are mixed.

REFWORLD: *World Directory of Minorities and Indigenous Peoples: Jamaica*, also on the Internet, quotes the 2006 Census as well, with the figure of 90% Black, and people of mixed heritage with combinations which include: European-African, Afro-indigenous, Chinese-African and East Indian-African. They add: "There are also small, well established minority populations of Lebanese, Syrians, Cubans, Europeans and South Asians."

One might think that the people came from their lands with specific inherent interests and skills; can it be mere coincidence that so many grocery stores are owned and operated by Chinese Jamaicans, while jewelry stores and gift shops by and large are run by people of East Indian descent?

An indigenous and distinctive Caribbean instrument, the steel drum.

But no description of the island can be complete without mention of Jamaica's music. It is remarkable that a country roughly the size of Connecticut (146 miles long and only fifty-one miles across at the widest point) has influenced music throughout the world.

Chiefly through Bob Marley, but followed by the likes of Harry Belafonte and Jimmy Cliff, the music, originally Calypso which had migrated from Trinidad, and later Reggae and Ska, has spread worldwide. Perhaps this very music is the uniting factor that keeps the island country with its largely impoverished population, so and vital and alive.

12 PATOIS

Jamaicans love to talk; talk about the government, talk about their girlfriends or boyfriends, talk about the weather, taxes, their neighbors, anything, and to anyone. And I've known at least one Jamaican who talks to himself if there is no one else around to talk to.

Jamaicans refer to the everyday language most of them speak, as 'Patois,' and this Patois is the mixture of African and English that grew out of the original language of contact. Linguists call that language 'Pidgin.' 'Pidgin' is the language that was spoken spontaneously by the people, most of whom were brought to Jamaica from the western part of Africa, and the English speaking plantation owners or foremen for whom they would be working. 'Patois' or 'Jamaican Creole' as linguists call it, is the language that evolved from that original 'Pidgin.' It is the language that has been passed on to subsequent generations and is the language that is spoken by most Jamaicans.

However, that having been said, almost no one in Jamaica speaks 'pure' Patois today. Most people in Jamaica speak a blend of Patois and 'Standard English' (SE). Some linguists speak of a 'continuum' which stretches all the way from the kind of Patois that is totally unintelligible to visitors on the island, to SE as it would be spoken on the radio or on TV. Frequently an individual will speak at more than one level of the continuum, that is, communicate in different mixes of Patois and SE, depending on circumstances. A Jamaican who works in a bank, a hotel or a shop that caters to tourists, might, when with family or friends, speak a language close to the Patois end of the continuum; might speak something midway between Patois and SE with fellow workers; and might speak something closer to SE with customers or guests on the island.

All this makes Patois sound rather chaotic or haphazard, but it has its own grammatical rules, which have been put forth in Beryl Bailey's wonderful book, 'Jamaican Creole.' Without getting too technical in formulating the rules, one can say: Patois [generally] does not use the verb 'to be' in the present tense; past and future are indicated by 'were' or 'wi,' respectively. Many plurals are formed by adding 'dem' to the singular; and 'articles' are seldom used. If needed for clarity, 'a/an' becomes 'wan' while 'the' is rendered as 'de.' Pronouns for the most part do not distinguish case and gender, usually a simple 'im' stands in for 'he,' 'she,' 'it,' 'him,' 'his' and 'her,' while 'dem' takes care of their plurals. Many word endings are omitted. But once, when speaking with Vera I said, "me foot-dem hurt", she corrected me. "No, mo-oms! You mus' say "Me FEET hurts.""

Sometimes, in an effort to speak SE, a Jamaican may hypercorrect, that is, use an inappropriate term or grammatical construction as an approximation of what sounds to him or her like the Standard English that visitors speak. To cite an example; one day I reminded Paulette, the helper we'd hired to do laundry after we'd moved to the apartment, to be sure to turn off the pump when she finished. She assured me, "I don't forgot!" Another time when rain was about to fall, I asked her if the sheets on the clothesline had dried. "It don't perfect," was her response.

But no matter on which level of the scale between the two extremes, a Jamaican will always speak with the charming pronunciation and distinctive lilt that is so typical of Jamaican speech.

Some Jamaicans incorrectly refer to their Patois as 'bad' English. But there is no such thing as a bad language or a good language. A language is a language.

One of the characteristics of Jamaican speech is a very broad 'a' sound accompanied by the dropping of the 'r' sound. This is similar to the speech used in Boston, where they speak of 'Haavaad Yaahd,' for example. A couple from Massachusetts, Connie and Johnny Woodward, used to spend six weeks in Jericho each winter, and they frequently spoke of going to Maaablehead [Marblehead, a resort not far from Boston]. When Vera first heard this 'aaah' sound from Connie she was shocked. "Me nebber hear no white 'ooman [woman] taahk so baahd!" she exclaimed.

Another characteristic of Jamaican speech is the dropping of the 'aitch' sound at the beginning of words spelled with the letter 'h,' and adding an 'aitch' sound to words beginning with a vowel. This 'Cockney' type of pronunciation is heard on many levels of speech, almost all the way to SE. Thus, while you will always hear offers of 'honions' or 'horanges' at the marketplace, you may also be offered 'am and heggs' for breakfast by a dignified waiter in an elegant hotel dining room.

One time Janney wanted to make bean soup, for which he needed a ham hock. Realizing the likelihood of confusion since 'ox tails' are often used in the local cuisine, I told the butcher I wanted 'smoked hocks,' the kind, I said, that are pigs' legs, not the kind that's from a whole huge animal like a cow. The butcher just laughed, telling me, "Us doesn't has neigh-der!"

When Vera spoke of 'hushers' at a wedding she'd attended, I could clearly imagine the formally attired groomsmen cautioning the guests to keep the chatter down.

Yet another feature of Jamaican speech that you may sometimes hear, is the pronunciation of 'ow' as 'oo.' I was in a butcher shop one day, a real one where they wait on you, when Mr. Witherspoon, an Englishman who is a year-round resident of Ocho Rios, was waiting for his order of a half dozen pork chops and a large bag of 'Bow Wow,' a local brand of dog food that's frozen in slabs and then sawed up into slices. Yvonne, the daughter of the shop owner, brought out the dog food first and laid it on the counter. "My word!" exclaimed Mr. Witherspoon, "those pork chops certainly look GOOD!"

Yvonne, chuckling, asked, "Do you mean to tell me, Mr. Witherspoon, that you can't tell the difference between pork chops and Boo Woo?"

* * * * * * *

One night, some time after we'd moved out of Jericho and into our Jamaica apartment located on the second floor of a two-story building ['upstair house,' in the Jamaican parlance], I woke up to a rumble of thunder and flashes of lightning. Quickly closing our bedroom windows I went to check on the guestroom. And there I saw a head, silhouetted by another flash of lightning, and a hand reaching through torn screen for a trinket on the dresser top inside. I reached for the light switch and the head and the hand instantly disappeared from view, accompanied by a loud thud below.

I awakened Janney who called Hurley Whitehorne, our friend and lawyer who lived with his wife Dorothea, in an apartment below. Hurley came running up brandishing a sabre, followed by his friend John Williams who was there on a visit from Kingston. Prior to his and John's retirement from the Force, Hurley was a Colonel in the Jamaica Defense Force, with John as his Major. With the same sabre at his side, Hurley had led the troops to welcome Queen Elizabeth II, when she visited the island, and more recently, Janney and I had watched as Hurley used the same sabre to cut the wedding cake at his and Dorothea's wedding. By now the intended thief was long gone and nothing had been stolen.

The real culprit, it turned out, was the very tall ladder which someone had left lying around on the property unsecured after a roof repair job. The plan now was to secure the ladder by chaining it to a nearby tree until someone could figure out what to do with it. I was elected to buy the chain.

Arriving in the hardware store I told the clerk that I

needed sixteen feet of chain. The man simply ignored me, staring off at something beyond my left shoulder. They're just not used to women in hardware stores-- men's domain.

"Chain," I repeated, linking my fingers together. "I need sixteen foot of chain!"

"Oh, mos' be 'chyen you want," he said, still indifferent. "Us doesn't has no sixteen foot o' chyen," he said as he turned away.

"But what are those?" I asked, pointing to several large wheels with 'chyen' rolled up on them. "I want to buy sixteen foot 'o chyen! What DO you have?"

"Us has chyen fe go-at, chyen fe pohppy, chyen fe dog and chyen fe coo."

"How long is chyen fe coo?"

"Sixteen foot."

Mission accomplished.

13 CRICKET, LOVELY CRICKET

Jamaicans love their sports! In these, just as in the continuum in Patois, there are great differences among the various social and economic classes, but cricket is the most popular sport by far, as well as being the most democratic. In one form or another it can be enjoyed at any level, while sports such as golf, polo or off-shore game fishing are of necessity reserved for those with deeper pockets.

Cricket is taken very seriously and nearly every village has its own team which plays on a regular basis against friends or neighbors in another village or nearby parish. And the game is enjoyed on another level by those who bet on it. Betting shops are dotted across the island and anyone who wishes to do so can wager his money on dog or horse races as well as on major local or overseas cricket contests.

Janney and I, along with George Peace, a friend who worked with Janney, tailgated at a neighborhood cricket match one afternoon while George was visiting us. As the game progressed, I understood almost nothing about what was going on, but there were just enough similarities with baseball so that I THOUGHT I might eventually understand--I didn't!

Granted--there are two alternating teams of eleven, one of which bats while the other fields the ball; so far so good. A man on the fielding team, the 'bowler', runs a few steps swinging his arm all the way around several times before throwing the ball underhand. A cricket bat is shaped like a large spatula, its flat side about 4 inches wide, and just as in baseball, the batter runs after hitting the ball, but this is where all similarity ends. The batter carries his bat with him as he runs to the 'crease' where there are three stumps; these are the 'wicket'. Another batter now bats, and after hitting the ball, he also runs carrying HIS bat to the other end of the 'crease.' This continues over long periods of time, both runners running in opposite directions along this 'crease,' rather than completing a circuit as they would in baseball. They are trying to prevent the ball from reaching the 'wicket' by swatting at it with their bats. As many as a hundred runs [called a 'century'] or even more may score during one 'innings' (not 'sic'). This first 'innings' might not even be completed before darkness descends, in which case the same 'innings' will resume the following day before the opposing team ever even comes to bat. An 'innings' ends when ten batters are 'dismissed.' Since there are always two men running, I don't know what becomes of the eleventh.

Janney first heard his favorite, 'The Victory Calypso' in Barbados in 1950, soon after the 'Windies' [West Indies team] surprised everyone by defeating England in a 'Test,' which corresponds to the World Series, lasting five days. The Test took place at the 'Lord's Cricket Grounds' in London. The Victory Calypso 'Cricket, Lovely Cricket' was quickly composed, with numerous verses covering every phase of the Test;

"Cricket, lovely cricket, at Lord's where I saw it. Cricket, lovely cricket, at Lord's where I saw it. Yardley tried his best, but Goddard won the Test ... " for example, each stanza or verse ending with the same chorus:

... *"Those two little pals o' mine, Ramadhin and Valentine."* celebrating two young bowlers who are credited with having won the last match.

*   *   *   *   *   *   *

The next day, a Saturday, we took George to watch polo. George had been having some family difficulties back home and we wanted to cheer him up so he would forget his woes and enjoy every moment of his stay. Polo in our area was started by a now elderly

British couple, whose name I believe was Cotter. They at that time presided over each match, living high up over the town of St. Ann's Bay. It is said that on a clear day they could see Cuba, some ninety miles distant.

THE POLO SET AT UPTON.

The players are mostly local business people who own their own polo ponies; John Collier and his wife Jill being very noticeable among them. Their horses were frequently seen grazing on the sweet, green grass of the Upton Golf Course.

A game consists of six 'chukkas,' seven minutes in length, with three minutes in between (five minutes at halftime). The four players on each team try to hit the ball between the goalposts using a long handled mallet, while at the same time preventing the other team from doing so. Time-outs are called only in the case of serious physical injury or danger to horse or rider such as a loose saddle or lost helmet; otherwise the player can leave the field to change horses during the course of play (30 or 40 horses may be involved), or in the case of a broken mallet, simply hit at the ball with the handle end. Polo is a fast moving game. At half-time and at game's end, spectators are encouraged to go out on the field, which is nine times the size of a football field, to replace the divots that have been churned up by the ponies' hooves. Even the Queen of England has been known to engage in 'divot stomping'.

Polo, which has been described as a cross, somewhere between hockey and chess, was brought to the island in 1890, the St. Ann's Bay club [called Drax Hall for the estate on which it is located] is the oldest original club in Jamaica.

At the time we attended polo, a sumptuous tea was presided over by Mrs. Cotter, who wore a slightly rumpled green chiffon frock and a wide brimmed hat crowned with a row of large roses. Small, very British looking children hovered anxiously, asking their mothers; "Mummie, might I have a bit of cake?"

* * * * * * *

While at the polo game, George overheard one of the spectators talking about a deep sea fishing expedition which was to take place on the following day. He expressed great interest, fishing being by far his favorite thing. Of course he was invited to go along, assured that the proper equipment would be available to him. He would be picked up the next morning at seven.

George was very excited and couldn't stop talking

about it and hardly slept that night. Up at the crack of dawn, he expressed his concerns. If he should happen to catch, say a marlin, or some other very large fish, how would he be able to transport it? Worried, he finally asked if we had a sheet in which he could wrap his trophy and strap it to the roof of the car. Vera located an old shower curtain as well some rope and George rode away a happy man.

His happiness, however, was not destined to endure; he never even got a nibble. When Janney and I went to pick him up and saw his dejected face, Janney spied another fisherman, carrying away a yard-long fish. For a small consideration, the luckier fisherman was persuaded to let George hold his fish while Janney snapped a photo. George, still not totally happy about how the day had gone, at least had a photo to take home to show his three sons.

GEORGE GETS HIS FISH.

14 BRAID YER HAIR, LADY?

Tourism is by far the most important industry in Jamaica, at least on the north coast, but sometimes the very people who stand to gain the most from it are their own worst enemies. Travelers who come to the island on cruise ships or by plane are literally besieged by those who want to show them 'the real Jamaica' (and sell them some pot), or sell them coconuts or other carved items that they say have a secret compartment (to hold pot), or take them to meet the 'real people of Jamaica' (who will sell them pot), I've heard of experienced travelers touring the Caribbean who refuse to get off the ship in Jamaica because they've heard they'll either be harassed or else won't understand what is being said to them. This is a shame; Jamaica is a beautiful island that has a great deal to offer (besides pot).

The Ocho Rios beach that we usually went to is a semi private beach--that is--there is a small admission fee of fifty cents, but whether it is fifty cents US or fifty cents JA is not specified. This is alright, the tourists assume it's US, while even the poorest Jamaicans can afford what amounts to around 16 cents. But this charge does not apply to everyone. People who are staying at certain hotels are waived this fee; the man at the gate mumbles a question as each person approaches, "Whey y' tay?" asked in a deadpan voice accompanied by an equally deadpan facial expression. I know this means, "Where do you stay?" or "Where are you staying?" He is asking this only in order to know whether or not he should charge them admission.

While this isn't actually 'harassing', this type of thing certainly does nothing to increase the tourists' enjoyment of their Jamaica experience. Why can't people who are specifically connected with the tourist industry be trained to speak so people can understand them? With something approaching 85% unemployment on parts of the island, surely someone can be found who can say these three or four words so they are intelligible to foreigners? To some tourists, especially those from a non-English speaking country, this can seem intimidating, or may even be frightening. They don't know if this is part of the bureaucracy or merely passing the time of day. These travelers have been showing documents to dozens of people everywhere they go and here is this man wearing some semblance of officialdom (a badge, epaulets or some insignia, though over a tee shirt and with flip-flops), asking them something they don't understand. When they don't respond, he asks the same question in the same way, but louder, "WHEY Y' TAY?" I used to become very angry with this young man. One day I was behind a couple who were German, I believe. That year, through some quirk in the system, exchange rates were extremely favorable for travelers from Germany--and they came to Jamaica in planeloads--so much so that one of the hotels even had notices posted in its lobby, which were headed: ACHTUNG!

The German couple ahead of me in line had their money out ready to pay; they became very concerned. The whole thing was just causing a delay for everyone, so I butted in. I'm not usually the pushy type, but this made me angry. "He is asking you which hotel you're staying in or if you are from a cruise ship." They understood me but still were worried about why he needed to have this information. Might it have to do with their visas?

So far I've only mentioned men doing the 'harassing'-- out on the beach it was a different story, or at least this was so in the past. There had been women on the beach, many women, large aggressive women, who wanted to braid your hair. My own hair was about three inches long and curled up tight with a fresh permanent, but still, three or four women would call to me and almost block my way, "Braid yer hair, Lady?" I don't know which came first; that is, if this practice started before or after the movie "10" came out. In it the beauteous Bo Derek jogged along the beach, her hair plaited in numerous braids with beads woven into them. It is really a wonderful idea. A woman could simply get under the shower after a day at the beach and be ready five minutes later to go out for the evening.

But too many people were complaining that they were being harassed by the numerous, very persistent hair braiders. They carried large baskets which blocked out the precious sunlight. Finally someone, the Chamber of Commerce or the Tourist Board, took a firm stand. The hair braiders were no longer allowed to solicit patrons on the beach.

But Jamaicans do not give up easily. Having stashed their baskets in the shade of a palm tree, the hair braiders would wade a few yards into the sea, and shouting, "Braid yer hair, Lady?" swim along coastline in the gentle surf.

15 The GLEANER

But no description of life in Jamaica is complete without mention of *The Gleaner*, Jamaica's premiere daily newspaper. I very much doubt that *The Gleaner* has ever had a proof-reader, although it certainly can use the services of one! The newspaper abounds with misprints, gar-bled headlines, mal-apropisms and photo headings that don't match the photos. The *New Yorker* magazine used to print some of the more amusing of these 'typos' that readers had sent in, but the misprints were so frequent (and so funny), that the *New Yorker* stopped printing them; thinking perhaps justifiably, that these bloopers were intentional.

A RECENT ISSUE OF
THE DAILY GLEANER.

No event is too insignificant, no detail too trivial for mention in *The Gleaner*. Though the paper is by no means a tabloid, the lurid frequently creeps in. Interviews of witnesses of criminal acts are quoted in deepest Patois. Many of the crimes reported are termed 'Praedial Larceny,' referring to crimes connected to the land. One frequently reads, "Man chopped for stealing goat;" a case when an enraged person, or perhaps an entire rural community has taken the law, and their machetes, into their own hands.

There is also a 'Tell Me Doctor' column alternating with 'Dear Pastor' in Monday's special supplement. Troubled Jamaicans write in hoping to solve their medical or spiritual woes. I remember the plight of one young lady whose family treated her 'like hog and goat,' complaining that she had 'only one-and-a-half pantie;' a bit hard to visualize, but so sad!

Beauty pageants and fashion shows are held frequently and reported in great detail, always pointing out how late they were in starting (they always are late). I remember a vivid description of a tomato flying through the air and landing with a resounding 'smack' on the shoulder of an unpopular contestant, while the audience hooted and jeered.

Beauty Pageant contestants are sponsored by various businesses and there is always a 'sashing' ceremony in which the young lady is presented with the ribbon she will wear diagonally across her chest, identifying her as 'Miss Pest Control,' 'Miss Al's Wrecker Service,' or 'Miss Brake and Radiator Repair,' for example.

I remember well an article in the Gleaner describing a wedding. The groom was owner of a plumbing business while the bride was a homeowner, planning to remodel her bathroom. A photo on the newspaper's front page shows them exchanging their 'I dos' in a bathroom. What could possibly be a more appropriate venue for their nuptials?

Another article describes a grizzly scene. The body of a woman has been found tied to a tree, her hands and feet bound, and she has sustained several stab wounds. The item ends with the statement, "Police suspect foul play."

* * * * * * *

I once placed a want ad in *The Gleaner*, offering Jericho for sale. Our rentals had not been going well due to political unrest. I listed our vacation home accurately as having 4 bedrooms and 4 baths, but the ad came out saying 1 bedroom, 4 baths. We received a number of responses, but not a single caller was interested in buying the house; they just wanted to know, "What for you want so much battroom?"

This reminded me of the time while we were still living

in Venezuela, when I put an ad in the *Caracas Daily Journal*, the English language newspaper published in the capital. What we wanted was to sublet our house to someone while we were in the States for our 'long leave' which would last two months. It was much better to have the house occupied, and obviously more economical than hiring someone to house sit. The ad was to run for ten days, so as to include two weekends. When my ad appeared with the wrong phone number, of course I immediately called the newspaper, asking them to please correct the number for the remaining time the ad was to run. They assured me that the wrong number would be corrected--possibly it was already too late for tomorrow's edition, but definitely it would be correct the following day. Surely the Señora would understand.

Well, the ad ran for the remaining eight days with the same incorrect phone number despite daily calls from me. Finally they agreed to run my ad for an additional ten days--free of charge--and of course with the correct telephone number.

It had the same wrong number again.

On the third day I called the incorrect number to apologize to those people for the inconvenience of all those calls I imagined they were getting. "No problem!" they assured me. They hadn't really planned on taking a vacation, but when these attractive offers came rolling in they decided it was such a good idea that they had chosen the best offer and were going to Aruba.

III. Living in the Upton Manner

16 LIVING in the UPTON MANNER

Upton Manor consists of two small apartment buildings nestled on the slope above the Upton Country Club [now Sandals]. The two 2-story buildings ('upstair house' in Patois), each with four apartments, were originally financed and built by a pair of retired Canadian businessmen, both as a vacation destination for themselves and their friends, as well as an investment.

It had once been quite stylish for the Country Club set to live or visit in Upton, but with the political unrest during Michael Manley's first term as Prime Minister [1972-80], and their own advancing age, the two businessmen decided to sell. One building was purchased outright as an investment by a retired couple, Sam and Lee Hart who lived farther up the hill in Upton; they would be renting out the units; while the apartments in the second building, some fifty yards away, were purchased by individual buyers, forming a loosely structured 'condominium'

Lee Hart, determined to restore a fashionable aura to the enterprise, went to considerable effort practicing her decorating skills; she ordered an elaborate brochure designed to captivate a golfing clientele. To her dismay, when the 250 copies of the brochure arrived, instead of 'Upton Manor,' the property was listed as 'Upton Manner,'

Between the time we purchased our Upton Manor apartment and the time we actually moved in, the whole population of the building had changed.

THE UPTON 'MANNER' APARTMENTS.

The husband of the middle-aged American couple in the unit below ours had beat a hasty retreat, just one step ahead of the entire Jamaican Constabulary Force who were determined to remove him from the island for 'Corrupting the Morals of Jamaican Youth.' He had been seen holding hands with a small black boy on the beach. His wife, without asking too many questions, also soon left after hurriedly selling the unit to, shall we say, a 'lady of easy virtue,' named Amber. So far-reaching were the attractions of Amber that even on days prior to her arrival, caddies and taxi drivers would come looking for her, already sensing somehow that she was near. She was sometimes accompanied by her twentyish daughter, Tiffani, who, well-anointed with coconut oil, sunbathed topless at a nearby beach, donning a bib while she lunched, every eye riveted upon her. Late afternoons the ladies would golf-- always wearing their high-heeled shoes.

The apartment next to ours had previously been rented out by its absentee owner to a pair of Pentecostal Missionaries. They had now been replaced by Gordon Walker, a young Canadian bachelor, who happily for us, was the manager of the Canadian Bank branch in which we did our banking.

The other ground floor unit, which formerly had been occupied by an Indian family, had always been accompanied by curried aromas which wafted through the breeze. Thoroughly aired out now, it was home to Hurlstone (Hurley) Whitehorne and the lovely Dorothea. Hurley officiated at our purchases of Jericho and more recently the Upton apartment, as well as the still ongoing sale of Jericho. He was a good lawyer, a good neighbor and we were lucky to have him for a friend. Dorothea, not so much.

But she knew EVERYONE and entertained frequently, often including Janney and me. One evening at a cocktail party Dorothea overheard a Costa Rican woman saying that she wanted to meet an American who spoke Spanish. Dorothea immediately invited the Señora for drinks the following evening, of course asking Janney and me as well.

As soon as we were introduced the Costa Rican woman addressed me in Spanish: "Señora," she said, "It is true, is it not, that when you Americans drink your Bloody Marys, you are drinking the blood of The Virgin?"

"No!" I quickly responded, "We are drinking tomato juice, vodka and a little Tabasco Sauce."

"But then, why do you call it 'Bloody Mary?'"

"It was named for an English queen who lived long ago."

"Ah! So she liked to drink blood?"

"No! She just liked to kill people. So they called her 'Bloody Mary.'"

The Costa Rican sniffed and walked away muttering "Ay, que locos son esos Americanos!"

In some other parts of the world, Hurley and Dorothea might have been considered an unusual couple, but not so in Jamaica. Hurley was descended from a long line of Englishmen in Jamaica, while Dorothea, with a quite dissimilar background, was the only child of a Jewish family who had been living in Germany. During the 1930s, her father wisely decided to leave Germany; it seemed like a very good plan. They moved to England while Dorothea was still quite young and English was her first language. So, brought up as an English miss, she married Ian, an Englishman who was studying horticulture. He found work in Jamaica investigating a blight which was attacking the coconut palms, and the couple moved to Jamaica.

* * * * * * *

In addition to his law practice, Hurley had been a Lieutenant Colonel in the Jamaica Home Guard since Jamaica's independence. He had served in what had previously been the Jamaica Reserve Regiment during World War II. At the time of our move, Hurley was married to his second wife, Audrey, who was Canadian, as the first Mrs. Whitehorne had also been. He was father to two daughters. Dorothea and husband Ian also had two daughters as well as a son.

Dorothea had taken a job in Hurley's law firm as office manager, and had eventually taken up residence with Hurley and Audrey in their country home in St. Mary, the Parish immediately to the east of St. Ann. By then, Hurley along with his two law partners had offices in Kingston, where he and Audrey owned an apartment, and in St. Mary as well as in Ocho Rios.

After her move into the St. Mary country home with Hurley and Audrey, Dorothea's husband Ian, along with the two daughters moved to the Cayman Islands, while the son moved to London.

Hurley was quite prominent throughout the British Commonwealth, frequently attending conferences and speaking at major functions. With his sabre at his side he had even led Jamaica's army, The Home Guard, to greet Queen Elizabeth II when she visited the island. Dorothea accompanied him on these occasions, in fact she took care of all the arrangements, freeing Hurley to indulge in the bonhomie he was so good at. But she soon tired of sitting at a distant table while the genial Hurley, natural in his 'hail fellow well met' persona, sat laughing and chatting with other dignitaries at the speakers' table. By this time he and Dorothea had moved to Upton leaving Audrey in the country home in St. Mary where she raised Pembroke Welsh corgis. Dorothea, fed up with the status quo, announced that she was not going on the important upcoming trip to New Guinea that summer unless she went as Mrs. Whitehorne. Nor would she make ANY of the arrangements for Hurley. This called for drastic action.

Reluctantly, Hurley began divorce proceedings from Audrey, with whom he was still on surprisingly good terms. He of course knew that pursuant to Jamaican law, he would be forced to relinquish half of his total worth to Audrey, including half of his law practice.

Doing so required him to sell the apartment in Kingston and the country home in St. Mary in order to buy out his 1/3 of the law practice in order to give half of that to Audrey, and to set her up in an apartment in Ocho Rios. This meant that Audrey had to give up her beloved corgis, and the small income they provided. Dorothea generously purchased one from the most recent litter, a snappy little creature that barked every time a telephone rang. Audrey's new apartment prohibited pets.

Janney and I attended the marriage ceremony that took place on the patio of their apartment. They cut the wedding cake with Hurley's sabre. Hurley, along with the new Mrs. Whitehorne, then departed for New Guinea.

THE MARRIAGE OF HURLEY
AND DOROTHEA WHITEHORNE.

Not long after their return, Dorothea became ill with multiple sclerosis, and was forced to retire from her position as office manager. Both Hurley and Dorothea have since died.

17 The SOUND and the FURY

We didn't go to Jamaica at all, the winter of 1994/95. Janney had not been well, but he was so much better by the following winter that we decided to take the chance. We flew down in the middle of December.

The telephone we had gotten for the 'condo' two years earlier and never had a chance to use was right where we had left it. Janney anxiously lifted the receiver; yes, there was a dial tone. He noticed that there was no pushbutton labeled '9,' but there were two '6's.' Okay, as long as it worked, although having been installed later, we had a different area code than most of our neighbors, making most calls, 'toll calls.'

Jericho has already had a phone when we moved in with an extension in the staff quarters. When we could not get one in the apartment, Vera arranged to have two guys from the phone company hang a wire as another extension of the Jericho phone. It worked for a little while, but then somebody found the wire and pulled it down.

We already knew we'd have to get an 'ICAS' number (a special ten digit identification number to dial), in order to make calls to the US. The Ocho Rios office of the phone company was the first stop on our agenda the next day.

Bright and early Monday morning, we pulled up in front of their building. I held my breath as I entered; there were only a couple of people in line ahead of me. Good! I didn't want to spend my whole first morning in a stuffy office when I could be on the beach. I could hardly believe it; we would actually be able to call family and friends in the States. However, this did not prove to be the case. Telecommunications of Jamaica had other plans for us; when it was my turn in line, the clerk told me that she'd be happy to take my application form but that I'd have to pick up the ICAS number the following week in St. Ann's Bay (temporarily the center of our universe).

We had waited twelve years to get the phone and two years to use it once it was installed; they had dropped it off earlier and come to hook it up just as we were leaving for the States. But at least we'd be in business by Christmas!

We had another stop to make before going to the beach to bake the Michigan chill out of our bones; and that was the Ocho Rios branch of the Royal Bank of Canada where we kept a Jamaican dollar checking account. During the two years we had been absent, the bank had added an ATM. Wonderful! I don't enjoy standing in line to cash a check either; especially on the days when a cruise ship is in the harbor and the bank is full of tourists cashing their travelers' checks. The ATM was outside the bank, built into its outer wall and surrounded by a thick plexiglass enclosure that could only be accessed with the ATM card.

Entering the bank I recognized one of the Customer Relations ladies, Mrs. McCauley. I got into the short line in front of her window.

While filling out the ATM card application form, I asked Mrs. McCauley if the same bank management was still in place. Though we'd had an account in the Canadian bank for nearly twenty-five years, every time a new manager came in we were given a hard time; we'd be told that we had to wait twelve weeks for our US checks to clear before we could draw on them, at which time we would already be back in Ann Arbor. We needed cash and we needed it now! Fortunately the same manager was still there and there would be no problem; I would be able to get some Jamaican dollars immediately. But my, oh my! The exchange rate now was 1 Jamaican dollars to $.38 US. $100 US provided a large pile of currency, but bought very little!

I asked Mrs. McCauley how long it would take to get my ATM card. "Two weeks," she replied. "We print the card immediately and then mail it to you. The mailing takes two weeks."

The Post Office, which stands on a corner, is right across the street from the bank--let's say 60 feet, though I think it's less. Hurley Whitehorne's office, where our mail is delivered, is right across the other street from the Post Office, say another 60 feet. The hypotenuse, or the distance from the bank to Hurley's office works out to about 85 feet.

The card never came.

Our Apartment Building
at Upton 'Manner.'

Returning to our apartment after the morning in 'Ochy,' we found the place in an uproar. A shiny, bright red pick-up truck was parked in the driveway and several young men were scrambling up and down tall ladders (not the one that was still chained to the tree), draping and looping miles of black cable over our balcony railings. Every dog in the area, of course, barking wildly. The scene reminded me of a Marx

Brothers' movie I'd seen when I was around 10 years old; 'A Night at the Opera,' in which Harpo, Zeppo and Chico clambered up the opera house curtain while Groucho wiggled his eyebrows and chomped on his cigar.

A neighbor, Chris, came over from the apartment building next to ours to tell us the good news; cable TV was finally coming to Upton! The existing TV service provided only two channels. For years there had been only one, the second channel having just been added a couple of years earlier. Chris told us the men were just putting in preliminary wiring but that service would begin in about ten days. The installation fee was to be Ja $800, or about 300 dollars US, and that it as well as the first month's rental fee of Ja $200 were to be paid now.

Not bad! We didn't even have a TV in Jamaica, but Janney and I talked it over at lunch and decided to bring down a small set when we returned the following winter. We would wait to get hooked up at that time. No point of paying that amount when we weren't even there.

The driver of the red truck came up and explained the system to us, collecting the installation and first month's rental fees from those who'd already sub-scribed. Saying he'd be right back he sped away. The other three man and the ladders disappeared as well.

We never saw any of them again!

They were thieves! The driver had been the mastermind; he'd stolen the truck with the rolls of cable, picking up some of his buddies to fake the installation while he collected the money. Our neighbors not only had been cheated out of their money, the men had also taken down their antennas, which they undoubtedly planned to sell to some other unsuspecting people. Our unfortunate friends had no TV service over the holidays, or at least until they could get a reputable firm to put up new antennas for them.

* * * * * * *

Arriving at the telephone company in St. Ann's Bay the following week, the clerk asked me all the usual questions. She consulted the application form I'd filled out in Ocho Rios a week earlier and punched the information into her computer. I was even prepared when she asked to see my passport--I had brought it with me. But I was NOT prepared when she asked: "How much calls will you be makin'?"

"Oh, I don't know; say three, I suppose."

Okay! We had our ICAS number, all we had to do is write down the number in some hidden place and we could call anyone we wanted!

On Christmas morning we talked to our daughter Kathy in Kansas and to Janney's brother Bill in South

Carolina and wished a Merry Christmas to Janney's sister, Peggy Jane in New Jersey, all the while marveling at the miracle of having a phone that worked. Once again, I dialed the ten digit ICAS number plus all the other numbers required to make an overseas call to my friend Patsy in Ann Arbor and all I got was a beep, followed by a 'canned' message which said, "We are sorry, your call cannot be completed as dialed."

Figuring I had made a mistake, I redialed the twenty or so requisite numbers; same message. I tried to call the phone company, though it was obvious no one would be there on Christmas Day. There wasn't. Nor the next day, Boxing Day, a holiday in Jamaica as it is in England. Next came Saturday, then Sunday--no one at the phone company, and the same canned message on overseas calls.

By Monday morning I was nearly apoplectic! I called the phone company at 9 sharp and miracle of miracles, a pleasant voice responded. I stated my business, asking, "what the *&%%#$" was going on. The woman on the other end of the line, after asking for my phone number, consulted her computer and then replied, "You are limited to three overseas call a day, and on December 25th, you attempted a fourth call. Your ICAS number has been deactivated."

My comments are perhaps best not repeated, nevertheless, the unfortunate clerk told me very politely that if I came to the office and filled out a form, I could get the number of calls allowed increased to five. The office in St. Ann's Bay, of course.

18 JOHN COLLIER:
the Czar of Upton

John Collier, the man who had brought the 'Dear Dad' letter to P.K. Saunders, is a character in his own right. At some time after that incident, Collier bragged to us that he had already known the contents of said letter by means of what he termed; "a bit of judicious steaming," and I suspect, a bit of careful planning for maximum impact. This would explain why he had arrived that morning looking like the cat that had swallowed the canary.

After the ownership had been transferred, Collier owned not only the Upton Golf Course (until it was bought out by the Sandals Hotel chain), but continued to own and operate the area's water, garbage and road maintenance systems as he had under P.K.'s aegis. And here we apply the term 'maintenance' loosely.

The entire water supply system at Upton had been deteriorating steadily over the years; pipes were corroding, valves were missing, there were numerous leaks. For some years frequent interruptions in water delivery had become such a nuisance that most of the permanent residents had either dug cisterns to collect rain water or had erected water storage tanks; large green, metal boxes on legs that dotted the landscape until forgiving vegetation concealed these eyesores. Gradually it became clear that water was coming through for only a few hours a week, so that even with a tank you still had to be very careful to ration the precious fluid. If your tank ran dry you could either phone Mr. Collier and risk his ire and sarcasm in the vain hope that he might pump a little water your way, or you could drive to St. Ann's Bay, about a half hour away and pay for a truckload of water to be delivered at some unspecified time in the future. There are those who depend entirely on trucked in water to fill their tanks, eschewing the Cascade Water Company, Ltd., Mr. Collier's system. The noisy trucks can be heard all day and late into the night, dragging a chain along the cratered road, constantly shifting gears, sloshing water up or down the steep hills of Upton, while every dog in the area barks ecstatically.

Collier maintained the golf course with the aid of a dilapidated tractor and a skeleton crew of two or three men. The tractor, which really belongs in an exhibit of ancient artifacts, served several functions. Usually driven by a Mr. Dunn, it pulled a fairway mower. Mr.

JOHN COLLIER'S ANCIENT TRACTOR.

Dunn executed intricate patterns as he cut the golf course grass, skillfully circling around a tree or a shrub before spiraling around the occasional cow that had wandered onto the course. Chickens ran about in the shade of a large mango tree on the seventh hole and a stray goat or two could usually be seen somewhere on the course.

At another time of day that same tractor might be seen towing an equally ancient wagon. Mr. Dunn would pick up a coup-

A COW LOUNGES IN THE ROUGH AT UPTON GOLF COURSE.

le of the caddies who might be loitering about the Club House, and set out to collect garbage, which had usually been set atop fences or walls, out of reach of marauding dogs; these dogs once more, all barking in unison.

MR DUNN OFFERS VERA A RIDE.

Mr. Dunn exerted great charm over the women of Upton; cooks and maids, many of whom would drop whatever they were doing and would rush out to chat with him. Mr. Dunn was very gallant; doffing his cap, he would make sweeping bows to one and all in the manner of a champion bullfighter. He generously offered rides on the tractor to anyone walking up or down the hill and generally radiated a spirit of chivalry and bonhomie, in addition to the aromas of his trade. Meanwhile, his helpers attended to the actual collecting and dumping of the trash, which would then be burned at a remote spot.

Road repairs, such as they were, were also carried out by Mr. Dunn, once more using the tractor and the wagon. A couple of barrelsful of marl, a sort of a clayey, sandy, yellow gravel, would be tossed into the wagon and Mr. Dunn, working solo now, would pull up to one of the numerous and truly appalling potholes. Hopping from the tractor he would toss a couple of shovelfuls of marl into the gaping hole and stamp on it with his feet. Voila! Road repaired--until the next rain, that is. Then the marl would again be washed out and the road would be returned to its cratered state.

The only one who seemed happy with this arrangement was Mr. Dunn. The years had not taken their toll; twenty years after we'd first seen him he still looked wonderful.

In addition to the golf course, garbage collection, road repair and the Cascade Water Company, the enterprising Mr. Collier at one time also owned an abattoir, a stone structure which stood just outside the road to the golf course. This slaughterhouse provided Upton and the villages of Exchange and Lodge with unrecognizable cuts of beef from the scrawny cattle that munched lazily on the dusty weeds by the side of the road. Lucky were those cows that managed to get loose and feast on the fresh green grass of the golf course.

But even that is not all. Collier also had a Persian rug business. He kept his carpets rolled up and stored along the walls in the dusky interior of the abattoir (one hopes beyond the drip zone), until a likely customer happened along.

One evening (we were told this story by a long-time acquaintance of the Colliers), John was escorting a young lady, the daughter of a family friend, whom we'll call Francine, home from a party. John's wife Jill was off to visit one or another of their far-flung children: one in Australia, one in Moscow and the youngest, Belinda, still in school in England. Collier saw his chance and jumped at it. On the way back from the party, he invited Francine, who was evidently unaware of his reputation, into the abattoir to view his Persian rugs. Always resourceful, Collier had brought along a lantern. He showed the evening gown clad Francine into the slaughterhouse where he attempted to make his move; a struggle ensued. Francine freed herself and managed to hide momentarily behind one of the sides of beef which were now swaying gently from the hooks in the ceiling. She was thus able to make her escape and limp away up the road in her strappy sandals.

As we know, Mr. Collier has now sold his golf course; he has also divested himself of the water, garbage and road repair businesses. The abattoir has long since crumbled into a picturesque ruin, but who knows? Perhaps somewhere, the now gentleman of leisure is still showing his collection of Persian rugs to unsuspecting young ladies.

19 WATER, WATER, EVERYWHERE

As we have seen, for some years the water supplied by the Cascade Water Company, Limited, one of Collier's enterprises, was becoming even more limited than before. You never knew when (or if) the water might come on--in the middle of the night or when you were away, but it was seldom on for more than two hours of a 24-hour period. When it actually did come on, the whole building would shudder, as surprisingly strong pressure sent water CASCADING through the starved, rusty, pipes. After a season of trying to keep the bathtub and several bucketsful of the precious liquid stashed here and there, we finally admitted defeat and decided to do what the permanent residents had long since done; have a tank put up. Even though we spent only a portion of each year in Jamaica, we were approaching the age when we would both retire and be able to stay the entire winter. If it performed as promised, (not everything in Jamaica did), the tank would fill when John Collier, who WAS the Cascade Water Company, turned on the valve and water came churning and rattling its way through. We could then pump this water up to our second story apartment.

Collier manipulated the maze of pipes and valves concealed somewhere on his hilltop property, channeling water to whichever part of Upton he felt deserved it. Aside from John, and possibly his daughter Belinda (when she was in residence during vacations from school in England), there was only one human being who knew how the 'system' worked, and he was a Jamaican golf course employee, whom Collier, for some reason, called 'Scotchman', though he was anything but a Scot. Scotchman drove up and down the fractured roads of Upton in a golf cart, listening patiently to complaints from housewives, cooks and maids in those homes that still subscribed to Collier's service.

The terrain on which our apartment building stands has a very irregular contour. Built, as are many if not most constructions in Jamaica, it rests on a very steep slope. The building's northern elevation enjoys a panoramic view of what is now the Sandals Upton Golf Course and the blue Caribbean beyond, while its south side looks out across our driveway and up the fern covered bank which rises vertically above it, some 12 to 15 feet high. The slope then continues over what once was a vacant lot, before finally emerging through trees and shrubs onto the Upton road.

Surveyor's pegs showing our building's property lines had been located above this fern-covered rise, several yards beyond the top of the driveway which bisects it. Our building's clotheslines were up there, almost hidden from view, along with some flowering shrubs and a few wild orchids that were tucked in here and there for the pleasure of our co-owners. This was the view from our bedroom windows.

On the recommendation of our friend and neighbor Hurley Whitehorne, a well-known Jamaican lawyer who was highly respected throughout the island, we hired a Mr. Beam as the contractor to put up our tank. Mr. Beam, after viewing the situation, suggested putting the tank above the driveway on that upper level, in order to take advantage of 'gravity flow' during the (frequent) power outages. Instead of erecting one of those green metal eyesores that dot the landscape and that would dominate the view from the upper-story windows of our apartment building, he recommended putting up a stone structure next to the large mango tree that was close to the property line. This would be attractive and picturesque and could have colorful vines growing around it.

These power outages were fairly commonplace. I well remember a three day Easter weekend without electricity. Some idiot had tried to steal a mahogany tree from a nearby estate and the tree had fallen, pulling down all the power lines in the area. I felt sorry for the women who had planned to bake a traditional Easter fruitcake called 'bun' [but pronounced 'bon' as in 'bon jour'], which they gave as gifts to friends and neighbors, and of course their Easter dinners would be ruined if they depended as we did on electricity. Many Jamaicans cook on charcoal, but you can't bake cake on a barbeque.

With the absence of electricity, Janney and I were having Campbell's vegetable beef soup for our Easter dinner. Janney had fired up the small hibachi we had on our verandah and the soup had just begun to bubble merrily when along came a carefree little lizard, tripping blithely atop the railing. Suddenly, the lizard began to dance--a puzzled expression on its small

ANOLE LIZARDS CHANGE COLOR, BLENDING INTO THE BACKGROUND.

green face. The railing was hot from the hibachi, and the poor creature lost its footing, dropping straight down into our soup.

I was unable to face any aspect of the situation, but Janney took the saucepan down to the yard, depositing

ALL its contents behind a tree. It was a long time before I could even look at that saucepan--but I digress!

* * * * * * *

Eventually our tank was ready. A rare and beautiful flowering vine called the 'Jade vine' for its blue-green blossoms was planted at all four corners in hopes of covering the tank's sturdy but unbeautiful cinderblock foundation. But we still had no water and we were expecting houseguests the next day. The tank needed to be filled, and the debris in the water then had to settle out before it could be used. I realized that I was leaving myself open to scathing sarcasm, but I picked up the phone and dialed Collier's number. Belinda answered! We were in luck! She said she would try to send some our way.

Late that night we were awakened by the glorious sound of water gurgling and churning into our new tank. The water coming out of our faucets the next day was a bit gritty but at least we and our guests could shower and flush toilets when they got there. We boiled all the water we used for cooking and drinks and made sandy looking ice cubes, but buoyed by several glasses of rum punch we and our visitors managed to survive.

20 The CAMPBELLS ARE COMING, HOORAY, HOORAY

In the meantime, the property across the driveway and immediately up the slope from us had been sold. The new owner, Lloyd Campbell, was a Jamaican who had lived and worked in New York City for over thirty years. He was about to return to Jamaica to live, bringing with him his wife Cathy, a Chinese woman from Hong Kong.

Before starting to build, Lloyd had his lot surveyed, and a new property line was established. The clotheslines, our water tank and the flowering shrubs, were found to be on Lloyd's property, along with another water tank that our new next-door neighbor, Hurley's friend John Williams had built. John, who was an Englishman, and his Jamaican wife Regna, continued to live and work in Kingston, planning to use the

Upton apartment as a weekend getaway. Janney and I pleaded with Hurley to try to purchase the small strip of land our tank was on, but we were assured by all parties concerned that it would take years to do so, and of course by then it would be too late.

Soon, steel posts were cemented into the ground. Before our worried eyes, a ten-foot high chain-link fence was erected all around the property line, encircling the flowering shrubs and our two tanks; the clotheslines had quickly been moved to more neutral ground.

Of course we had been complaining all along to Hurley, who could see for himself what was going on; but he, as our friend, neighbor as well as our lawyer, said that Lloyd was completely within his rights, and advised us to wait and see what happened next.

Now a concrete slab was being poured right over the roots of the huge mango tree that stood above the bank of ferns, just inside the chain-link fence. If the tree were to fall, it would completely obliterate any vehicles in the driveway and do SERIOUS damage to our building, especially the upper story apartments. The Campbell's gardener told Vallen, the gardener shared by the tenants of our building, that Lloyd was planning to put up a 'three-bedroom doghouse' on the slab. Sure enough, a few days later two Dobermans and a German shepherd appeared in Campbell's yard.

A 'trainer' visited daily, apparently to train the dogs to be vicious. We could hear him taunting the dogs and shouting for them to "Bite! Bite! Bite!"

The Campbell's house seemed to be nearing completion. It was built high up at the very top of the slope; so extreme was the slope that the dogs down by the fence-line couldn't even see the house, much less would they see or hear a thief who might be planning to break into the house at the sides or at the front near the road. The dogs stayed close to the fence overlooking OUR property and barked ferociously anytime that anyone came onto it, a rather frequent occurrence, since eight households were accessed by our driveway.

There were also three dogs living on OUR side of the fence and of the driveway; two next-door and one in the other building.

One of the dogs in OUR building barked anytime ANY telephone rang; whenever ANY of the dogs barked, the other five would join in.

By looking at what we could see of the back of Campbell's house through our windows and at the front from the road we could see fourteen windows, and no two were alike. Some were casement, some double hung while others were clerestory, but all were different sizes and shapes.

Wily John Collier (we were speaking now that our

water situation had improved despite the unfortunate placement of our tank) suggested that Lloyd C had ordered the house plan from a newspaper or a magazine, which had merely shown examples of a variety of window styles as possibilities, but that Campbell had taken the plan literally and ordered one of each kind as shown on the drawing. He had gone to enormous expense. All furniture, fittings, appliances and construction materials other than sand, cinderblocks and cement, had been containerized and shipped down in a crate the size of a railway boxcar. Digging down into the rocky formation had made construction of the house and its large pool proceed much more slowly than anticipated. The house was three stories high with two huge wings jutting out obliquely to embrace the pool. Entering the home from the pool was a large room with a vast glass door-wall where some sixteen tables, each surrounded with chairs, were set up in case of inclement weather during a pool party or other outdoor activity.

At about the time the Campbells were moving into their dream-home, John Collier announced that he was getting out of the water business at the end of the year. After a good deal of soul searching, we and the owners of the other three apartments in our building, decided to build a large cistern, or underground water tank which would be fed rainwater running off our roof during the rainy season. We would need new gutters or eaves troughs to route the water from the roof into one or more pipes and down into our huge cistern. Each apartment would then require an additional pump to raise the water from the cistern into our individual tanks. The existing pumps would continue to pump water from each of our tanks into our respective apartments. The start-up cost would be great, but at least we would no longer be paying the substantial yearly water fees to Collier.

The cistern was built in due time, the new pumps installed and the new gutters had been hung. Then the rains came and the cistern was filled as planned.

* * * * * * *

One Sunday afternoon, the Campbells, who were now living in their monster house on the hill, came to pay a social call. We sat for forty-five minutes or so and made pleasant chit-chat as we sipped the drinks we had offered, speaking pleasantly of the weather, the gardens, the gardeners and so on. Then, just as they were rising to leave, Cathy began to shriek at me, saying that we must take down our pump, that it was making her sick! Of course she was within her rights; the tank WAS on their property, even though it wasn't visible from their house. The jade vine had pretty much covered it, and I was quite certain the pump was out of earshot--we couldn't hear it and we were closer than they were. When I asked her if John Williams' pump, which was identical and not more than three feet away from ours, was also causing a problem, she said, "No. His doesn't bother me". I told Cathy we would remove the offending pump as soon as possible. "No!" she screamed. "Now!"

We never turned the pump on again, relying on gravity flow until we found a Mr. Donovan who promised to make the second pump, pump water directly from the cistern to our apartment, but it never worked properly from that day on. Instead of cutting on when a faucet was used and cutting back off afterward, we had to go into the kitchen to flick a switch on the wall each time we needed to flush or to brush our teeth and then go back to turn it off; otherwise the pump would just keep on pumping and in time would burn out.

We had spent a substantial amount of money on the tank, on our share of the cistern, and of course on the two pumps, but still did not have a satisfactory water delivery system.

Besides boiling the water used for drinking, cooking and washing fruits and vegetables, we had also brought with us, on the advice of Janney's doctor in the States, a filtration device which worked by osmosis. This was to purify the water that ran into the cistern from the large roof, visited frequently by birds and other fauna.

I rued the day I had ever set foot in Jamaica!

At about that time we heard through the grapevine that Lloyd Campbell was planning to sue the Cascade Water Company, Ltd., for failing to provide water for his household (Campbell had made no arrangement prior to building for acquiring water for his kitchen, five bathrooms and pool); and that John Collier was planning to sue Lloyd Campbell for helping himself to some sod from a property he (Collier) owned.

At least there was no talk (yet) of the Campbells suing us for having a water tank on their property, and Cathy hadn't (yet) demanded that we tear it down. Oh what a mess that would be, not to mention the considerable expense!

21 JAMAICA FAREWELL I:
EARLY MORNIN' TEA

So, here we were in Jamaica again. We had a phone and could make five long distance calls a day if we wished, but our water situation was still far from satisfactory! We'd tried several different plumbers but no one could make the pump work as it should.

* * * * * * *

Prior to our trip, Dr. Martha Gray, our family doctor in Ann Arbor, suggested that we take along the most recent part of Janney's chart recording his vital statistics. This would establish a 'norm' or a 'baseline' in the event that something went wrong. Her main concern was his creatine level, since he had suffered renal failure briefly following major surgery three years earlier. We contacted Dr. Tomlinson, a doctor we knew in the area, soon after our arrival in Ocho Rios. After a brief examination, we left the paperwork with him.

Janney had been doing quite well health-wise but suddenly, early one morning in mid-February I was awakened by a loud thud--Janney was on the floor. He had fallen getting out of bed and was flailing around helplessly. When I reached to help him it was instantly clear to me that he was very ill; he was burning with fever and soaked with sweat. While not exactly unconscious, he was totally unaware of his surroundings. Nor, as we later learned, would he have any recollection of the incident. It was good that we had a phone. I called Hurley Whitehorne; he and Dorothea came right up, also routing out John Williams who fortunately happened to be in residence at the time. Together, the men got Janney back onto the bed while Dorothea hurried to phone Dr. Tomlinson. She told me his home was nearby; it was still early and luckily she caught him before he'd left for his office in town. He arrived presently and after a brief examination told me that Janney would have to go to the hospital. Not to the hospital in nearby St. Ann's Bay, but to University Hospital in Kingston. He arranged for a nurse come to our place before we left for Kingston; she would draw blood in order to establish a new baseline for Janney's creatine level.

The University of the West Indies is spread out over

several islands, Barbados, Trinidad and Antigua as well as Jamaica, but the University's Medical school is in Kingston. University Hospital there has a special wing, the Tony Thwaites Wing, where 'everything's up-to-date;' Janney was to be a patient there. The wing had been funded by and named after a man who was concerned that people in Jamaica requiring serious medical attention were going to Miami instead of University Hospital.

I was relieved that Janney was going to Kingston, even though it meant an hour-and-a-half drive on winding mountain roads. We'd heard horror tales about the hospital in St. Ann's Bay. We heard that patients in the maternity ward slept three to a bed, that there were no sheets or pillows provided; that you had to bring your own towels, washcloths, soap and toilet paper as well as the sheets and pillows, or you had none. And unless you brought your own cup, you couldn't even get a sip of water. We'd even heard a firsthand report from a woman who'd been having a heart attack, but it couldn't be properly diagnosed because nobody could find THE (that is, the ONLY) stethoscope the hospital owned.

Dr. Tomlinson made arrangements for an ambulance to take Janney to Kingston, telling them to bring two strong men. Janney would have to be carried on a stretcher, down the steep steps from our apartment. Dottie, our helper, and the nurse arrived minutes apart, followed some time later by the ambulance--in fact, two ambulances pulled into the driveway in tandem. A young woman who was staying at one of the hotels in Ochi had suddenly taken ill and was going to the same hospital as we were. The drivers of the two vehicles, both good-sized men, managed very well, carrying Janney down the steep concrete steps on his stretcher. I grabbed my handbag and got in, while Dottie quickly handed me a parcel. Then, with a whoop and a holler, lights flashing, sirens screaming, both vehicles sped from the driveway, gravel spitting from under eight spinning wheels. We were off for Kingston--all six dogs were barking ecstatically.

I sat in back with Janney, who was oblivious, along with a male nurse named Iggy. The driver was introduced to me as Dr. Crooks, but Iggy called him 'Professor'.

* * * * * * *

I had plenty of time to reflect on the 'ambulance stories' I'd heard when we first came to Jamaica. A polo player who had been injured during a polo match near St. Ann's Bay had been rushed to the nearby hospital in that city. Once there, the doctors, finding they were unable to cope with the injuries he had sustained, referred him to a hospital in Kingston. On the way to Kingston, the ambulance was involved in an accident in which the polo player was killed.

In another case that had been described to us, the back doors of the ambulance had swung open going up a steep mountain slope on the way to Kingston. No one noticed. The patient, gurney and all, slid out the door. We never heard the outcome of that one.

* * * * * * *

We'd gone about fifteen miles when we heard the rhythmic slap, slap, of a flat tire. Fortunately we were on relatively level terrain. The other ambulance waited as Dr. Crooks and Iggy put on the spare, then we were off again. We got to the top of Mount Diablo without further incident and were heading down its far side. We'd just reached the place where the road drops off precipitously, curving down to the underwater bridge across the Rio Cobre, when both our vehicles slowed to a crawl. Looking out the back window, I could see car after car behind us, stopped on the narrow, really only about one-and-a-half lane wide, road. However, with both our sirens blaring, we were just able to creep through. We later heard that there had been a horrendous accident there and that cars were backed up over two miles in either direction.

About then I noticed Iggy shaking out a thermometer. "What's my husband's temperature, Iggy?" I asked.

"One hundred and five," he replied calmly. "One hundred and five?" I asked in panic. "One hundred, point five," said Iggy patiently.

* * * * * *

Iggy and Dr. Crooks spoke quietly with one another; the headache I'd had earlier had settled into merely dull throbbing; Janney's breathing was even and he did not stir. I reflected on the Spanish place names encountered throughout the island, the only vestige of the Spanish settlers who had eradicated the peaceful Arawak population. They, in turn had been defeated by British troops in 1660, in what was called 'The Battle of Rio Nuevo.' This was one of the two places Columbus had landed on his first trip to Jamaica, and was close to the beach where WE had bought lobsters on OUR first trip to Jamaica, some twenty-six years earlier. The present-day population of the island calls the place 'RY'n'vo.'

'DR SIR' RPG CROOKS

AMBULANCE SERVICE.

PHOTO COURTESY OF *THE GLEANER.*

I had completely lost track of time when we suddenly coasted to a halt; the sound of our siren droned into silence; the light stopped flashing. Looking out the back window once more, I saw that the sky was dark and a sea of headlights surrounded us. We were obviously in Spanish Town or Kingston, but why had we stopped? Were we near the hospital? But I could hear the other ambulance's wailing siren fading away in the distance. Iggy got out and spoke with Dr. Crooks, but I couldn't hear what they were saying, and then-- nothing happened. We just sat.

After what seemed like a half a century, I again heard the sound of a siren; this one approaching. I could still hear the men talking in front, but I couldn't make myself heard to ask my numerous questions. Finally the other siren came close and an ambulance came screeching to a halt in front of us. Dr. Crooks and Iggy lifted Janney, still on the stretcher and still not relating to the outside world. They put him into the ambulance that had just arrived and motioned for me to get in. Once again we went screaming off into the rush hour traffic, eventually arriving at the hospital.

Now Iggy explained to me that the vehicle we had been in had completely lost power and that the driver of the other ambulance, realizing that we were in trouble, had continued to the hospital, discharged his patient and then come back for us.

"Weren't we lucky the other ambulance came back to pick us up?" I said to Iggy. "Oh no problem," he replied, "Dem both belong to Professor."

* * * * * *

On entering the hospital, we were greeted at the door by Dr. Henriques, a tall, imposing figure of a woman. She was the administrator of the Tony Thwaites Wing where Janney was to be a patient. Dr. Paul Scott would be in charge of Janney's case, she told me. Dr. Scott had been waiting for us for some time, but had gone home to have some supper. He would return at nine.

I asked Dr. Henriques if there was any place I could stay overnight. There was no way I would go back to Ocho Rios leaving Janney incommunicado, only to return in the morning. I knew exactly four people in Kingston, the Millers and the Williams, both couples friends of the Whitehornes. But the Williams were in Upton at the moment, and I had no idea how to reach the Millers. Dr. Henriques told me that it was strictly against policy, BUT, under the circumstances and due to the lateness of the hour, instead of the private room Dr. Tomlinson had ordered, they would put Janney into a double room which was vacant, and I could stay THAT ONE NIGHT, in the second bed.

Dr. Scott finally returned. He kidded me a bit about being so late (he'd heard the whole story from the driver of the first ambulance; the flat tire, the delay on Mt. Diablo and the engine failure). After a brief examination he ordered an I.V., blood tests and an antibiotic, all of which were administered by a sweet, young nurse in a crisp, white uniform. It was only then that I sank, gratefully, onto the narrow, white hospital bed and fell sound asleep. Fourteen hours had passed since I'd found Janney in distress.

At five o'clock the following morning I was awakened by a hoarse little voice in our room, croaking, "Early mornin' tea. Time to wash op for early mornin' tea! Where is your rog?"

Light from the corridor partially illuminated our room; I could just make out the figure of a small man. "Rog?" I asked stupidly, still not fully awake and like my Wonderland namesake, not quite sure where I was or what I was doing there. "Wash rog! Wash op for early mornin' tea." "Don't want any! Go away!" The little man shrugged his shoulders and left, impatient with ignorant foreigners who didn't know what a 'rog' was and who didn't want early mornin' tea! But it would be four hours till breakfast was brought in.

At seven o'clock a nurse came in, also crisp in starched whites, carrying a wash basin in one hand and a pair of towels in the other. "Where are his rog and soap?" she asked, gesturing toward Janney. He was still not responding.

I remembered the package Dottie had handed me as I'd gotten into the ambulance. Dottie had been right on! Besides slippers and neatly folded pajamas, the bag held two towels, two wash cloths, a bar of soap and a roll of toilet paper. We were in business!

While the nurse ministered to Janney's needs, another woman entered the room. She wore a yellow rayon dress with large turquoise and black flowers printed on it. Introducing herself as the dietician, she asked, "What do you want for breakfast?" Janney, though still not with it, shook his head, "No." I, on the other hand, could have eaten a horse! I hadn't eaten anything in at least a day and a half. I assumed Janney was getting nutrition as well as his meds through the I.V. I'd have to ask to make sure. Breakfast, as were many of the meals provided, consisted largely of thick slabs of yam [yom]; not the dainty yams I bought in cans in the States to make candied 'sweet potatoes' for Easter dinner, but huge hairy tubers that grew under Jamaica's tough reddish-brown soil.

*　*　*　*　*　*　*

Janney was hospitalized for five days, during which time I remained in the room with him. Nobody seemed to care; the staff just took me for granted.

June and Paul Miller came to visit; very welcome guests, bringing with them very welcome books. Dorothea had phoned, telling them of our plight. John Williams, who had returned from Upton, was also very welcome when he came to call, treating me to ice cream in the hospital canteen.

Though I scrubbed the little 'rogs' after each application, I was concerned about the sanitary aspects of cleansing an entire person with the same, now threadbare, cloths.

Each morning the little man came in at 5 am, chirping about 'early mornin' tea,' and each morning I shooed him away. By the time Dr. Scott discharged Janney, he was able to walk out of the hospital and sit up in the taxi that took us back to Upton. No more of Dr. Crooks and his ambulances for us.

Janney didn't remember anything about the ambulance ride there; in fact the only thing he did remember about the whole five days was the little man with his 'early mornin' tea."

* * * * * * *

Before we left, Dr. Henriques told me that she would be billing us for expenses incurred during Janney's hospitalization, through Mr. Whitehorne's office. This was good. I would have to transfer US dollars to our Jamaican checking account. I would also try to find out if any of the costs would be covered by Blue Cross/Blue Shield or by Medicare.

Deciding to phone the American Embassy to find out, I looked in the Yellow Pages of the Kingston phone book, and found 'Embassy' between 'Embalming' and 'Embroidery.'

22 JAMAICA FAREWELL II: WON'T BE BACK FOR MANY A DAY

A few days after our return from Kingston, I was walking though the Ocean Village Shopping Center on my way to the bank, when I noticed that the glass storefront where the Ocho Rios Laundromat had formerly been was now painted black--but was completely covered with white lettering. Stepping closer, I read:

HOLISTIC MEDICAL CENTER

Dr. RPG Crooks

Mrs. PJ Crooks, Nurse

In addition to 24 hour Ambulance; Rescue service; the sign proclaimed:

GENERAL MEDICINE (COMPLEMENTARY)
HOMEOPATHY * BOTANIC MEDICINE
ACUPUNCTURE (CHINESE MEDICINE)
CHIROPRACTIC / OSTEOPATHY
(BACKBONE DISORDER)
ORTHOPAEDIC SURGICAL PODIATRY /
CHIROPODY (FOOT)
SPORTS & PHYSICAL MEDICINE
(PHYSIOTHERAPY)
PSYCHOTHERAPY * HYPNOTHERAPY
REHABILITATIVE MEDICINE
CLINICAL MEDICAL EMERGENCIES (24 hrs.)
DIETETICS & NUTRITIONAL MEDICINE
MEDICAL LABORATORY

Now at least I would know where to get help, no matter what was troubling me!

* * * * * * *

Janney had been gradually regaining his strength, when suddenly about a month after his hospital stay, he once again began to run a fever and sweat profusely. Of course I called Dr. Tomlinson immediately. He came that evening and prescribed an antibiotic, warning me that if Janney's temperature did not return to normal in three days, he would have to go back to the hospital. Our friend next door drove to Ochi to pick up the prescription for me, for which I was very thankful.

I am happy to say that the fever dropped rapidly and that he recovered soon from this latest set-back. I was seriously considering going back to the States as soon as Janney was well enough to travel. We had tickets for our return trip on April 14th, more than three weeks away. Leaving early would put us right into the Easter/Spring Break rush, which meant crowded conditions and frequent delays, not exactly a good time for a sick man to travel, even should we to be able to get our reservations changed.

At that point I told Janney that I was not coming back to Jamaica. I'd had enough; it was too hard! In the US, I'd only have to dial 911 and help would be on its way in minutes. We talked it over when Janney got better. I had heard that there were people looking for homes in Upton now that the Golf Course was under Sandals' management. Predictably, Janney was reluctant; he really loved Jamaica, but after a few days he gradually came to the same conclusion. We decided to put our apartment up for sale and to clear out as scheduled on April 14th.

We hired movers to pack the beautiful cabinet Janney'd had built for his cassettes, as well as the few items we wanted to have shipped to Ann Arbor. Our very good friend, Pat Moyers, had a Yard Sale for us at her place. We got appraisers in to do an evaluation in order to set a sale price; we arranged to have painters come in as soon as we left. I gave Dottie tons of clothes for her church and--whew! The two-and-a-half weeks flew by; all was in readiness and it was time for us to leave.

* * * * * *

Two days before our departure, the Campbells came to pay a social call. Again we chatted about this and that; health matters, the weather, and so on. And once more, as they were rising to leave, Cathy began to shriek, "Alice! Alice! You must take the tank down! You have to take the tank down NOW! BEFORE YOU LEAVE. And Alice! You must guarantee that the jade vine will not be damaged!"

Only one slender stalk of the vine remained; a hurricane the previous year had torn off the other three shoots. But that one remaining strand had spread out to envelop our tank completely, along with the mango tree and most of the Williams' tank as well.

I told Cathy there was no way I could guarantee the safety of the vine-- in fact, I could almost guarantee that the vine could not be preserved if the tank were torn down. Cathy said she was counting on me.

NURTURED BY THE LUSH, TROPICAL ENVIRONMENT, THE JADE VINE COVERS THE WATER TANK.

I reminded her that this was Friday, and that we were leaving early Sunday morning. As she went out the door and started down the stairs, she turned and shouted, "Then you must have your agent protect the vine!"

Janney immediately telephoned our friend, neighbor, lawyer, Hurley Whitehorne. Hurley came up that evening and we discussed the situation over drinks. Hurley, who of course would continue to live there after our departure, and would continue to be the

Campbells' neighbor (and perhaps THEIR friend and lawyer as well), called a meeting of the five of us--himself, Cathy and Lloyd Campbell, and Janney and me--for 9 o'clock the following morning, Saturday, our last day. We would meet at the foot of the tank.

I woke up early the next day. The sky was dark, rain was pouring down. I wondered, vaguely what shoes to wear--most of our things were already packed. At 9 am the phone rang. It was Hurley, calling to tell us that Lloyd Campbell was ill; the meeting had been called off. They were going to use the tank to supply water for a small house they had decided to build for their gardener, down by the fence (not far from the three bedroom dog house).

* * * * * * *

(And though the meeting did not occur, I still cannot not shake off the picture in my mind: a picture of the misty gray morning, five people standing in the rain, heads bowed, huddled under black umbrellas dripping into the grave--err, I mean the tank ... A REAL HOLLYWOOD ENDING!)

ABOUT THE AUTHOR

Once again, Alice Rainich Nichols shares tales of her adventures around the world, in the midst of a fascinating, and unfamiliar culture. A breath of Caribbean breeze touches this collection of heart-warming, humorous tales, related so colorfully with Alice's keen ability to capture moments of human kindness, joy, and weakness.